Every Month Original
Novels, Stories, and Articles

MONTHLY

USA Today Bestselling Writer
Dean Wesley Smith

TABLE OF CONTENTS

SHORT STORIES

FULL NOVEL

SERIAL NOVEL

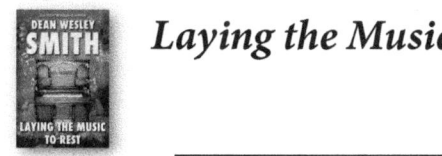

NONFICTION

Smith's Monthly Issue #34

Introduction
COLD POKER GANG

One of my favorite series to write is the twisted mystery series starring the Cold Poker Gang. And in this issue is yet another novel set in Las Vegas with the retired detectives trying to solve cold cases.

The key with the Cold Poker Gang is that what seems like an impossible cold case sometimes turns into really complex and ugly larger crimes.

I had a fan of this series last week ask me where I came up with the crimes in this series and I honestly told him, "I don't know."

Not a clue.

I just start off each book with what seems like a logical cold case, actually a standard cold case that face police in cities all over the world. I try to make the victim real by showing them on the day he or she vanished.

Then I jump to the present and have the detectives not only interacting with each other, but trying to solve a case that often has been cold for a decade or more.

From there I just let the detectives follow the clues that come up.

And I have to admit, I cheat some. All of the detectives I write about, even though retired, have ended up with vast resources in one way or another.

Not only are they retired and thus don't have to follow exact procedure or do paperwork, but they have the money and they know computer people who can really dig at information.

Where this idea came from was simple. It was a wish-fulfillment. I wondered what it would be like for very experienced detectives in a large city like Las Vegas to have all the time in the world to focus on a cold case and all the resources in the world to focus at the case as well.

No reality there at all and I know that, but that one nod to a fantasy situation allows these retired detectives to really dig at the underside of crime in many ways.

Thanks for the Support

Dean Wesley Smith

And I hope make the puzzle entertaining to the readers who like that sort of thing.

A number of people have said that the Cold Poker Gang would make a fantastic television series and I agree, it would. In fact it's sort of designed that way.

But they are also the types of books I would want to read and I learned a long time ago that if I didn't entertain myself, I wouldn't entertain any of you.

So I put the Cold Poker Gang up against impossible cases and then just entertain myself letting them try to figure it out as I try to figure it out at the same time.

Hope you enjoy the novel. I had fun writing it.

—Dean Wesley Smith
Lincoln City, Oregon
July 11, 2016

The Cold Poker Gang Mysteries
Now Available from all your favorite booksellers in trade paper and electronic editions.

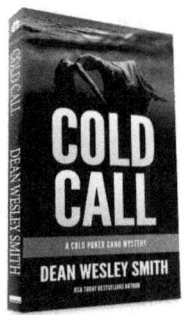

Coming Next Issue in *Smith's Monthly*

STAR FALL

A Seeders Universe Novel

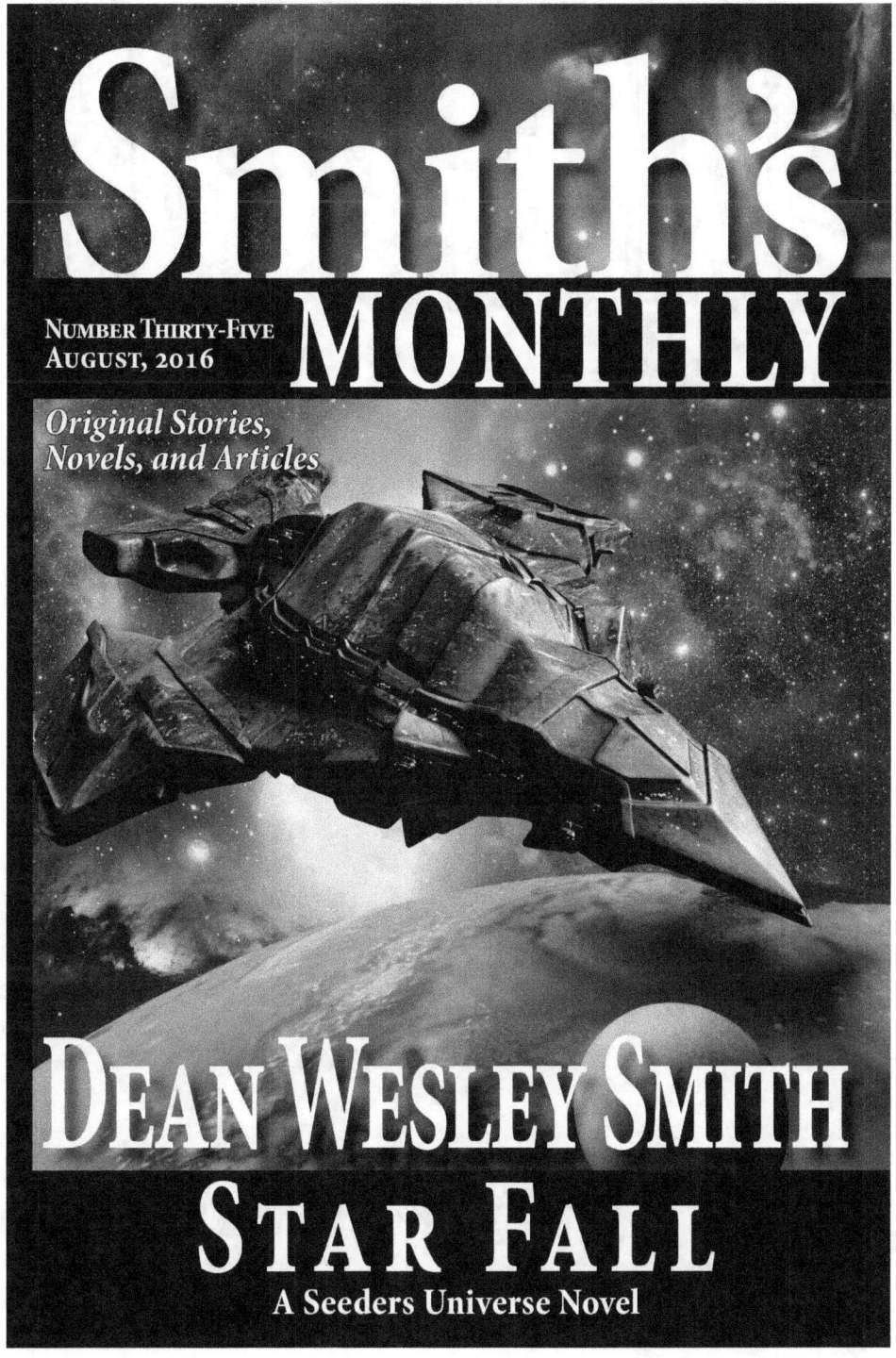

Smith's MONTHLY

NUMBER THIRTY-FIVE
AUGUST, 2016

Original Stories, Novels, and Articles

DEAN WESLEY SMITH

STAR FALL

A Seeders Universe Novel

POKER BOY
WMG
DEAN WESLEY SMITH

EARTH'S GREATEST USA TODAY BESTSELLER WRITER

APPROVED BY THE COSMIC CASINO
PANTHEON

POKER ♠ BOY
♥
♣
♦

NO. 32

WORLD'S FINEST POKER SUPERHERO

the LIBRARY of ATLANTIS

Poker Boy specializes in asking stupid questions. But sometimes even stupid questions need answers.

To save the fabric of all things from unraveling, whatever that means, Poker Boy must go to the Library of Atlantis and do something that no one ever accomplished before.

Poker Boy saves all things. Again!

THE LIBRARY OF ATLANTIS
A Poker Boy Story

ONE

"THERE IS A god of the Internet?" I asked, knowing instantly that my blurted out question was flat stupid. Of course there was, there was a god for everything that existed it seemed.

Stan, the God of Poker and my direct boss, just gave me the look he always gives me when I have asked a question beyond my normal stupid. Then he shook his head. He had on his usual gray sweater vest, gray slacks and open shirt, also a non-color. Stan was the dullest dresser I had ever met and he never altered what he wore.

Of course, I wasn't much better considering I only wore jeans, a dress shirt, a black leather coat and a fedora-like hat. I considered the coat and hat my superpower costume. Stan shook his head every time I mentioned that as well.

Patty, aka Front Desk Girl and my girlfriend, patted my leg and laughed lightly. She had her long brown hair pulled back and had on a wonderful white blouse and tan slacks. She had added color to the outfit with a turquoise necklace and earrings. When she patted my leg like that, I knew the question was beyond stupid.

I started to ask who it was, then just shut my mouth and decided one foot in my mouth at a time was enough, especially right before lunch on a warm summer's day.

The three of us were sitting in the large diner booth in the center of my office. My office was invisible and floated about a thousand feet above the Las Vegas strip. It had four glass walls, which made the view of the desert and subdivisions and mountains surrounding Las Vegas just stunning. And at night, the lights of the city were fantastic.

Patty and I liked to come up here at times and just sit with our feet up on the wood railing around the entire office and stare out at the stars above and the lights below. Just saying, that view had started many a romantic evening.

Besides a few chairs, the only furniture in the square room was a replica of a diner's booth with a tan Formica tabletop and a red vinyl bench seat that wrapped around three sides. At the moment, Patty and I were sharing a vanilla milkshake in a tall glass and Stan was working all by himself on a massive chocolate milkshake that he seemed to be studying more than drinking.

Madge would be bringing us lunch shortly. She was a superhero in food service and owned the diner in downtown Vegas where my team used to meet. When this office was built, we put in a connection to the diner from this office that she uses to bring us food and drinks. And team members without teleporting powers use that entrance as well.

Madge liked having us up here in this office better than in her restaurant, since we didn't clog up a booth for regular customers and didn't spook people by teleporting in and out all the time. She said it had been like expanding her restaurant by one table without all the costs and construction problems.

Suddenly Ben appeared in front of the table. Ben was the oldest-looking god I had ever met and looked like anyone's short, balding grandfather, right down to the too-large suit jacket and pants that didn't match. His brown leather shoes looked like he had bought them a hundred years ago and never even dusted them off.

He had been the God of Lamplighters, but as that profession faded, Stan and I saved him, got him to join my team and also got him a new job as one of the Gods of Books and Libraries.

I considered Ben our brains. Because his job for centuries had been so dull, he had been an avid reader of every text he could find, and he could remember everything, and I do mean everything, no matter how many centuries ago he had read it.

"Join us," Patty said, smiling at Ben and motioning for me to scoot over which I did. Lunch in my office often turned into a team affair and I honestly liked that.

Ben shook his head. "Got a problem."

At that, Stan seemed to come back into his eyes and pointed to the open spot beside Patty. "Sit and tell us about it."

Ben nodded. Then as he slid in, he said, "Maybe I should tell Laverne at the same time."

At that point my warning bells were going off in full seven-alarm mode in the back of my mind. Laverne was one of the most powerful gods in the world. She was also known by the name Lady Luck.

"Laverne?" Stan said into the air, slight worry creeping into his eyes. Stan had a perfect poker face. Me being able to see worry on it just made my alarm bells ring louder.

Patty touched my leg and I calmed some. She had the wonderful gift of being able to keep me calm through just about anything. I loved that superpower of hers.

"Right here," Laverne said, appearing and pulling over a chair so she could sit at the end of the table. She had on her standard gray silk business suit. Her hair was pulled back tight giving her thin face a stark look and the entire outfit made her seem even more powerful than she was, if that was possible.

She turned to Ben. "So what's the problem?"

"The Library of Atlantis," he said, looking distraught.

Stan sat forward, clearly worried.

Laverne did the same.

I wanted to ask how Atlantis could have a library since the entire continent sunk a whole bunch of centuries ago, but decided now was not the time for my second really dumb question of the day.

"Is there something wrong at the library?" Laverne asked.

Ben nodded. "Very wrong."

If I didn't know better, I would have sworn old Ben was about to burst into tears. He normally was the coolest, the calmest of anyone on my team.

We all stayed silent until Ben took a deep breath, gathered himself, and looked directly at Laverne.

"A book is missing."

Now, if this had been April 1st, I would have fallen out of the booth laughing. And luckily for me, I didn't even snort because Patty, Stan, and Laverne were acting as if this really was the end of the world as they knew it.

"How is that possible?" Laverne asked.

"I don't know," Ben said. "None of us do. It just isn't possible, yet it happened."

"It can't happen," Laverne said, her voice almost angry.

When Lady Luck got angry, you didn't want to be anywhere around.

"We know that," Ben said. "But it did happen and that's why I came here. We searched everywhere. This is a last resort before the entire fabric of everything we know starts to unravel."

Unravel?

Fabric of everything?

Now he had my attention.

TWO

I SAT THERE silently, something fairly unusual for me, as Laverne and Stan peppered Ben with questions about what he and the other Gods of Books and Libraries and all the superhero librarians working for them had done to find this missing book.

It seems they had looked everywhere. They had searched all recently filed books in case the missing book had been misfiled.

Then they had done the unthinkable to Ben. They had run an entire inventory of the entire library, physically checking to make sure every book was in place with no extra book anywhere.

It seemed the book had left the library and that was a very, very, very bad thing for reasons I had yet to figure out.

Finally Laverne stood. "We need to go to the Fates."

With that, she and Ben were gone.

"We are so screwed," Stan said, going back to staring at his milkshake.

At that point Madge came in carrying our lunch. She had on her typical too-tight pink uniform with a white apron that I swore had stains on it from the last century. And she always wore far, far too much makeup for any human face.

She looked around and frowned which managed to not crack her makeup. "I thought Ben and Laverne were here as well."

"They were," Patty said. "They had to go. There is a problem at the Library of Atlantis."

Madge set a wonderful-smelling cheeseburger in front of me nestled on a basket of fries. She gave Patty her club sandwich, and then Stan his cheeseburger. She might look the part of a back-road waitress gone to seed, but she was the best short-order cook I had ever had the pleasure to meet.

"So what's the problem at the library?" she asked.

"A book is missing," Stan said, his voice low.

Madge sort of froze in mid-step. Then she looked back at Stan.

"You are kidding, right?"

"Nope," Stan said.

"We are so screwed," Madge said, heading for the entrance to the diner.

That was enough for me. I needed some answers and I needed them fast, no matter how stupid my questions sounded.

"Stan, could you jump and tell Screamer we are having an emergency meeting. Have him bring Sherrie."

He nodded and vanished.

I turned to Patty. "I'm going to need to ask more than my normal number of really stupid questions here very soon if we're going to help with this. Stick with me, all right?'

She nodded.

At that moment Stan came back. A moment later Screamer and Sherrie appeared.

Screamer was about my height at six foot and wore jeans and a dress shirt and a light sports jacket. He normally worked for the police because his main superpower was the ability to get into people's minds with a touch.

Sherrie was Screamer's wife and worked as a superhero for food and beverage tending bar in Reno. She was also one of Lady Luck's four daughters. Today she had on a short black skirt, a white blouse, and an apron with the name of a casino on it. Clearly she had been at work.

"So what's emergency," Screamer asked as Stan let him and Sherrie scoot into the booth and then took his spot back in front of his untouched milkshake and cheeseburger.

I nodded to Stan and he said simply, "A book is missing from the Library of Atlantis."

Sherrie just turned white and her hand went to cover her mouth. Screamer shook his head and repeated what Stan and Madge had said.

"Now, time to fill in the new kid on the block," I said. "First off, someone please tell me what the Library of Atlantis is?"

"It started as the great library of Atlantis," Stan said. "All the knowledge of the world from the time of Atlantis was stored in that great building."

"When Atlantis was destroyed," Patty said, "no one wanted to see all that knowledge go away, so with the help of hundreds of gods, the Gods of the Library protected the library with a vast dome sort of like this office, a half-turn out of phase with the real world."

"So where is this located now?" I asked, fearing that the answer would be under the Atlantic.

"Under about a hundred feet of rock in central Oregon," Stan said.

"Oregon?" I asked.

"It wasn't Oregon when they buried it," Stan said, not looking at me.

The Library of Atlantis was in Oregon. How strange was that? I would leave that bit of information until later to digest.

"So what is this library like now?" I asked.

"The problem came up about a century after Atlantis went down," Stan said. "The Gods of the Library decided since civilization was at a very low ebb, they would try to get at least one copy of every printed work in existence in the library. All written human knowledge in one place. So they started expanding and after another thousand years or so, they managed the task."

"Damn dumb idea," Screamer said, shaking his head.

"So what happened when they got all written human knowledge in one place?" I asked.

"No one really knows," Stan said. "Those a lot smarter than me say that it somehow tied together things about humanity that had never been tied together before, and created a powerful force that has been growing every century as millions more books are added into the library."

A couple things that I flat didn't understand, so I decided to ask the dumbest question first. "How does this library keep up with all the millions of books being published around the world today? And the electronic ones as well?"

"They just appear in the library," Ben said, a moment after he appeared in front of us. "They are already sorted and filed and the library expands as room is needed

and the library shelves all of its own books now. No one ever really touches most of the books."

"Where is Laverne?" Stan asked as Ben sat down.

"Talking with the other gods who have been with the library from the beginning," Ben said, sitting down next to me in the booth. "They are all watching to see what will unravel first, try to stop it to buy more time."

"What is this unraveling?" I asked.

"From what I understand, you can think of it like a freeway," Stan said. "As long as all the traffic is moving along at the same speed, and the freeway can hold the number of cars at any moment, then nothing happens. But imagine one car suddenly stopping in one lane."

"A mess," I said. "So having one book missing will cause this?"

"And more," Screamer said. "It has never happened, but from what I'm told, a hell of a lot more."

Sherrie and Patty both nodded.

"And that's what is going to happen," Ben said, nodding. "It won't be pleasant for the human race and could set everything back by thousands of years."

"I hated the Dark Ages," Stan said.

I looked at him and made a note to ask him what exactly his job was in the Dark Ages. I don't think poker was in existence just yet.

"So this library is sort of magic," I said.

"Not magic any more than nature and weather or your powers are magic," Ben said. "Just a force. A human binding force that has helped us for centuries."

"So did you ever think of asking the library what happened to the book?" I asked.

Silence.

So I decided to follow up with two more dumb questions. "And what book

exactly is missing? And if no one touches anything anymore, how do you even know it's missing?"

Ben opened his mouth to answer, then shut it, clearly not having an answer to any of the three questions.

"Excuse me for a moment," he said, finally. He scooted out of the booth and vanished.

Seemed my three stupid questions might have hit a sore spot or two.

I glanced around at the four remaining. "Any of you ever seen this library?"

All of them shook their heads no.

I turned to Stan. "I don't have a library card, but I would love to see this place. Can you jump us there?"

He shook his head. "It's protected. Locked up tight."

Now that really bothered me. What was the point of having all written human knowledge in one place if humans couldn't even get to it?

That was one question I didn't think was so stupid.

THREE

"MIND CALLING LAVERNE?" I asked Stan. "I assume she could get us in the place."

"Why would you want to see such a vast repository of books?" Laverne asked, appearing in front of the table and again sitting down in a chair facing the table.

"Why do you keep all that knowledge locked away from the people who created it?" I asked. "Seems like the place shouldn't be called a library, but more like a book graveyard. It is underground, after all."

She frowned and said, "I don't know the answer to that question, but I will find out."

"Ask the library itself if it likes being locked away from people," I said, just as Laverne vanished.

Stan just shook his head. "As normal, your questions tend to get right to the heart of the problems."

"Only if no one knows the answers," I said, staring at my slowly getting cold cheeseburger and fries. My stomach was rumbling, but everyone considered this library thing a major disaster, so I figured that eating a normal lunch might be a little on the rude side.

I decided taking a sip of the melting milkshake might not be too far wrong, and maybe munching on a fry. I was just, deep down, having trouble taking one book being missing as a serious problem, especially since no one really knew what book it was that was missing.

A how-to-build-hydrogen-bombs book I might be concerned about, but a book on basket weaving, or a Zane Grey western would be another matter, even with this unraveling everyone seemed so afraid of, but had never seen in centuries.

I was about to take a second fry when I found myself standing near the center of a giant room, the polished marble ceiling towering far, far over my head.

I kind of choked down the first fry and gawked at the place.

The walls were at least three stories tall before curving up into the dome and were covered in dark wood bookcases, with walkways all the way around at every level, and the arches and pillars holding up the vast room were made of marble, polished to a shine.

The room had to be the size of a major college football stadium, and a hundred tunnels, at least, led off in all directions from this main room.

Stunning didn't even begin to describe this library.

The entire team was there, plus Laverne and Ben and a man in a long white robe with a long white beard I didn't recognize, but looked like he could have played the part of Gandalf in a Lord of the Rings movie.

We were the only ones in the big room, which could have easily held a thousand people and looked like it was originally designed for this big floor to have couches and chairs and places for humans to sit and read. But now the floor was just a vast expanse of marble, with patterns drawn in the center.

"I am Thoth," the robed man said directly to me. "The head librarian."

I bowed slightly as I always do in front of gods I do not know. They seem to like the respect it shows them.

I noticed that all my team, including Stan, also bowed slightly. This guy must really be one of the old ones.

"An honor," I said.

"You have made an assumption that we can talk with the entity that is The Library of Atlantis," Thoth said. "We have never done so, or even thought of doing so. Why do you make such an assumption?"

I didn't want to tell him I was known for solving problems by asking really stupid questions until one stuck. So instead I said, "It seemed logical. If you don't mind, I would like to give it a try."

Thoth looked puzzled and looked at Laverne, who nodded.

"Please," Thoth said.

I moved away about ten paces to the center of the large room. A pattern on the floor there told me that it was an important spot.

I looked around, then said simply, "Library of Atlantis, may I ask you a question?"

"You may, Poker Boy," a voice said in normal tones. For some reason I had expected some booming movie-god voice that would echo, but I guess this was a library after all and booming voices would be too disruptive, if they ever let anyone in here to disrupt.

I glanced back at Thoth and Laverne and the team. All of them were staring wide-eyed at me.

"May I ask how a book became missing from your wonderful vastness?"

"No book is missing," the library said. "I simply hid one book, *2001: A Space Odyssey* by Clarke, from the librarians to see what reaction I might get."

I laughed. "Seems you got a good one."

"I did, didn't I," the Library of Atlantis said.

I swore I heard it chuckling.

"Why did you pick that book?" I asked. I had seen the movie, but never read the book.

"I liked the voice of Hal in the movie. Would you like me to speak like Hal?"

I laughed. "Please, no. Too scary."

Again I thought I heard the Library of Atlantis chuckling.

"Why haven't you talked with the librarians before now?" I asked.

"No one thought to talk with me."

I glanced back at where Thoth stood. He had lived in this place for centuries and never once asked the library a question. Might be time for him to retire.

"You are the accumulation of all the knowledge in all these books," I said to the library. "Correct?"

"I am."

"And you are hungry for more knowledge which is why you take in all books being produced today," I said. "Am I correct?"

"You are."

"Do you wish the librarians would let others in here to use your collection and talk with you?"

"I do," the library said.

"Would I be welcome back to study the history of the gods through all time?" I asked. "I need all the help I can get on that topic."

This time the library actually chuckled. "Poker Boy, you and your team are always welcome here, considering how many times all of you have saved the world."

"Thank you," I said. "And thanks for not disrupting the fabric of everything. Or whatever happens when a book goes missing."

The Library of Atlantis just kept chuckling. Finally it said, "That's a myth. It was started back when I first became aware and no one ever asked me if it was true."

Now it was my turn to laugh.

Finally I decided to ask one last question of the Library of Atlantis. "One more question," I said. "It might be stupid."

"Poker Boy, I doubt if any question you could ask would be stupid. It might show lack of a certain tidbit of knowledge, but never stupid. And knowledge is why I am here."

"Thank you," I said. "I am going to remember that. My question is simply this: Is there a god of the Internet and who is he or she?"

"There is no god yet of the Internet," The Library of Atlantis said. "But if you want my humble opinion, someone really should take that job since the Internet is here to stay in one form or another for a time."

I glanced back at my team and just smiled.

Stan shook his head and Patty actually laughed.

"Thank you, Library," I said. "I hope to return soon to your wonderful halls and see them full of questing minds."

"I have that same hope," the Library of Atlantis said. "And Poker Boy, thank you for asking the right question. With gaining knowledge, that is often far more important than the answer."

"That's good," I said, laughing "because it seems I am never short of questions."

With that, the Library of Atlantis chuckled so loud, it actually did echo.

~

Now Available
from all your favorite booksellers in trade paper and electronic editions.

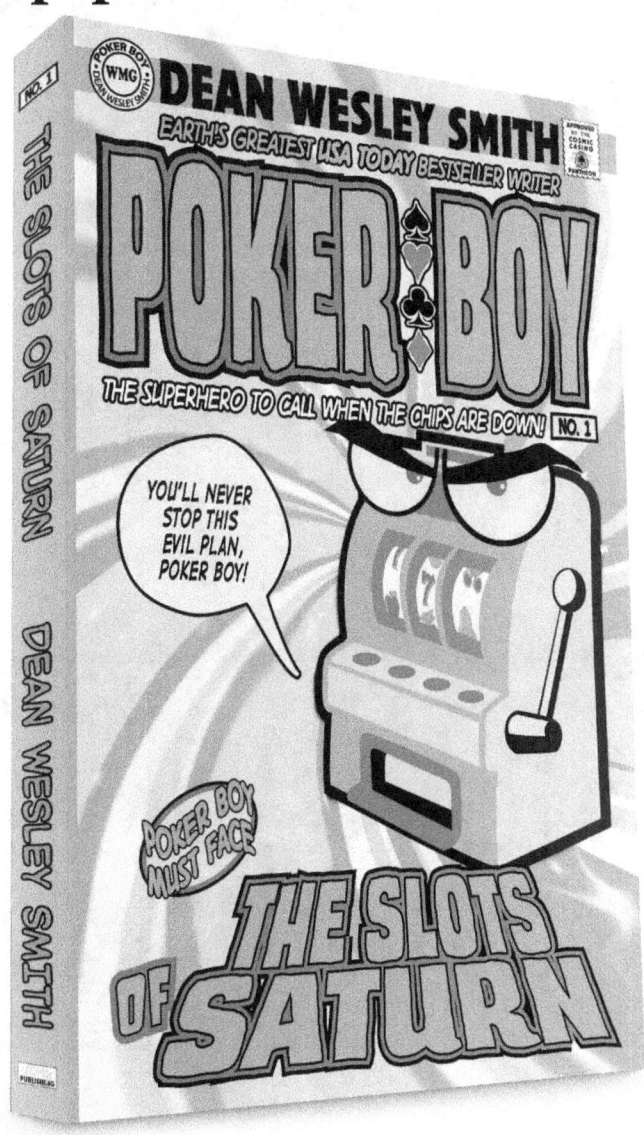

USA *Today* Bestselling Writer

DEAN WESLEY SMITH

START WITH A COFFIN

A Captain Brian Saber Story

Brian Saber awakes with a start in his nursing home room.

On missions, Captain Brian Saber defends the Earth Protection League in his warship The Bad Business. Tonight, he will be asked to do a very special mission without fighting.

But he loves any chance to be young again and help the League in deep space on the very edges of League space.

Swashbuckling space battles in deep space, fought as only those in the last days of their lives can fight. No alien finds safety around Captain Brian Saber.

START WITH A COFFIN
A Captain Brian Saber Story

ONE

CAPTAIN BRIAN SABER awoke with a start. The old clock in his nursing-home room ticked onward, ever forward, counting the seconds of his life draining away like a drip in a leaky faucet.

Faint moonlight colored the blinds white like ghosts hanging over the sliding glass door that led onto the patio in the center of Shady Hills Nursing Home.

With some effort, he turned his head enough to look around the small space.

Nothing had changed. Nothing ever changed in this room. One chair, one small dresser, his wheelchair tucked near the foot of his bed, and the guardrail up on the side of his bed as if he had enough movement in his old stroke-riddled body to turn over enough to even fall out of bed.

Through the open door beyond his dead legs and feet, he could hear a nurse moving around quickly. Something had happened in the hallway, but he had no way of finding out what.

So he just lay there, trying to listen.

He had no other choice.

He wasn't sure if he dozed or not because at his age, dozing happened pretty much without warning. But the next thing he knew, two men walked through his door. It seemed the commotion in the hallway had died down.

Brian instantly recognized one of the men as Lieutenant Kennison, the strong young man that carried him to the transport ship on nights of missions. Brian didn't recognize the other in the dim light.

Brian had just become a Captain in the Earth Protection League and he loved every mission he got to go on. But since last night had been a major mission, he hadn't expected another one tonight. There were usually a few days between missions, even though he wouldn't have minded going out into deep space every night to fight aliens and protect Earth.

The EPL had been formed by Earth centuries before, working with aliens friendly to earth to protect League Space. The only problem was that Trans-Galactic Flight regressed a body. It seemed that even though a ship could go faster than light, the physical body of a person inside regressed one year for every light year traveled.

So when Brian was put into deep sleep, he arrived at the frontier to defend the League Space often twenty-five years of age again. He had the memories of his old, stroke-ridden body, but the strong, healthy body of his youth.

And when he was returned to Earth, he was once again the old man who could no longer move around thanks to strokes.

He loved being young again. And he loved fighting aliens and saving Earth time and again. And because of that passion, he had risen to command his own warship, *The Bad Business*.

"Captain Saber," the man that Brian didn't recognize said. "I am General Drake of the EPL."

"I'm going to have to hold off on the salute, sir, until we get to the other side I'm afraid," Brian said.

The general chuckled and stepped a little closer. The general had to be in his late sixties. Nowhere near old enough to travel all the way to the EPL frontier. And he had the kind of face Brian liked and trusted. Not sure why, but the general felt like a good guy.

And besides, he had laughed at Brian's sad attempt at humor.

"We need your help on a problem," the general said.

"You know I am always willing to serve," Brian said.

The general nodded. "This isn't really a fight this time."

Now Brian was really confused. His job was to captain his battleship to stop aliens from invading over borders into the EPL space.

"What can I do?" Brian asked.

"You know Lester Watts?"

"Sure," Brian said.

Lester was a nice guy, warehoused two doors down the hall waiting to die like everyone else in this place. Brian and Lester often talked over lunch about family or friends. But mostly they had talked about fishing in deep lakes around the northwest when they were young. And they had both loved to fly fish on mountain streams.

At least, they talked over what passed for lunch in this place, since both of them had to be hand-fed. Lester had basically the same issues Brian had. The lower part of his body from his neck down was pretty much useless.

"Dr. Watts was a top botanist in his time, before his stroke," the general said.

"He never talked about that," Brian said.

"Tonight he had an episode and is going to die within a few hours," the General said.

Suddenly Brian knew exactly what was happening.

"You want to save him and take him out on the frontier where he can continue his work."

"That's right," the general said. "He was doing ground-breaking research and could really help us as we slowly expand outward to alien planets."

Watts was going to get the lucky card. He was going to get a second life out in space, where Brian and all his crew always had to come back to wait their time between missions as old people.

Brian had asked why at one point to his direct boss, General Craig, after a mission on the frontier that had the entire fleet working to push back an invasion.

The general had walked Brian over to a viewport and pointed to the three hundred large battleships and support ships that seemed to stretch off into the distance.

"Each of those ships has almost a hundred crew," the general had said. "And since Earth is not yet ready to learn about the EPL, we need secret crews to man these battleships."

Brian had understood at once. No way could thousands of elderly suddenly disappear from nursing homes and retirement villages around the world at the same time.

"And besides," the general had said, "it's cheaper for us to use large transports and take you all back to within minutes of when you left than house that many crew out here, where we have not yet been able to build anything we can defend for long."

That had all made sense to Brian. He hated it, hated being in his old body after spending weeks or months on a mission in his young body. But for now, his goal was to just stay alive when in the nursing home so if he was going to die, he could die in battle fighting to defend the planet.

Brian looked up at General Drake's serious expression.

"You need me to spend some time with Watts out on the frontier to explain all this."

"Exactly," the general said, nodding. "He knows you and you know what it's like to suddenly wake up young. I need you to keep him sane so he can go back to work. We'll transport him and your entire crew to *The Bad Business* near a frontier border and you all can show him around the frontier for a few weeks."

"I'd rather kill aliens," Brian said. "But I'll give it my best shot."

"Thank you, Captain," the general said.

He stepped back and saluted again.

"Wish I was going with you," the general said.

"I wish you were as well," Brian said as Lieutenant Kennison put down the guard on the side of Brian's bed and carefully picked him up.

"But we would have a problem if you did come with us," Brian said. "I can't change diapers."

Both Kennison and the general laughed as Kennison took Brian out his sliding door and into the cool night air.

A moment later they were drifting up to the hidden transport ship above. And less than a minute later, Kennison gently lay Brian into his sleep coffin, then stood back and snapped off a salute as the lid closed and the orange-smelling sleep gas filled the chamber.

TWO

CAPTAIN BRIAN SABER awoke what seemed like only a moment later.

He reached up and pushed open the lid of the sleep coffin and leveraged himself out with an easy movement, something he could have only dreamed about doing back on Earth.

He took off his old nursing home nightgown and tossed it in the coffin and then turned to his closet to get dressed. He was very familiar with this room, since it was part of his suite on his own ship. At some point, his sleep coffin had been moved from the transfer ship to his ship so he could wake up here ready to go.

He knew right now that the rest of his crew would be waking up and getting dressed.

He slipped on his tight pants, his silk shirt with long sleeves, and then his leather vest over his shirt with the EPL logo on the front. Then he pulled on his tall, leather boots and finally strapped on his wide belt with his two photon blasters, one on each hip.

He quickly combed his short thick hair into place with relish, since he hadn't had much hair on his head for the last forty years on Earth.

Then with one final look in the mirror, he turned and headed through his captain's suite and out into the hallway of his ship, turning to the right toward the bridge.

He had no idea where Dr. Watts was, but more than likely right about now Watts was thinking he was dreaming or going crazy or both.

Brian had thought the same thing his first time out here, and he had been briefed ahead of time. Dr. Watts, from his understanding, had not. They had simply waited until a stroke almost took him and brought him out here to save his life.

Brian walked into his small three-person bridge area and dropped into his chair. He was still getting used to the captain's chair, but it honestly felt right.

As he sat, Marian Knudson, a stunning redhead from a nursing home in Wisconsin came in and sat in the chair to his left. She was his second in command and the two of them had been on many missions before he had become a captain. And he had moved her to his second in command at once.

"Morning, Captain," she said. "Any idea what this mission is about?"

"We're a tour guide," Brian said. "Can you find where a Dr. Watts is located on the ship? He wasn't briefed before they yanked him and I need to see if he is even still sane."

"Major scientist?" Marian asked, her fingers moving over the screen in front of her almost faster than Brian could follow.

"I suppose so," Brian said. "We only talked about regular stuff back in the nursing home."

Marian nodded. "So you sort of know him. That's why we got the duty."

"Your guess is as good as mine," Brian said.

"Dr. Watts is in the main guest suite near the dining area on Deck Six," Marian said.

"Hold down the fort and see if you can figure out where in the EPL space we are exactly," Brian said. "I'm off to see what we face with the good doctor."

"Got it, Captain," she said. "Consider the fort held."

It took Brian five minutes to reach the doctor's suite, mostly because he stopped and talked a few times with members of his crew. Even though they were out here in deep space on serious business, often life-threatening business, every member of his crew considered this a vacation of sorts from their old bodies back on earth.

And he had to admit, he felt the same way exactly. But he also knew that these old people in young bodies would lay down their lives to protect the EPL space. And over the years, he had seen many die in battle.

When a person died out here, if the body was not too damaged, they returned it to within a minute of leaving the nursing home and eventually the nurse on duty would notice and the family would be notified and the body taken away and another old person would take the room, waiting to die.

In cases like Dr. Watts, they replaced his body with a dead clone body that looked identical. Or at least good enough to get through a funeral where embalming made anyone look like they were made of wax.

Brian knocked on Dr. Watts' door and got no answer.

So he used his Captain's override code to open the door and go inside.

He didn't know what he was expecting, but nothing wasn't one option.

He called out for Dr. Watts.

Nothing.

He keyed in his com-link back to Marian. "Thought you said the doctor was in this suite."

"Hang on, Captain," Marian said. Then after a moment she came back. "He is. He's still in his sleep chamber."

"Oh," Brian said, shaking his head and moving into the side room off the suite that held the sleep chamber. He went over to it and opened it slowly.

A young man with blonde hair and bright green eyes lay in the chamber in a stained nursing-home gown.

"Hi, Lester," Brian said. "You up for some fishing?"

Brian reached down and offered Dr. Watts a hand.

"Come on," Brian said after Watts looked like he might pass out from sheer fright. "Let's get you into some clothes so I can show you around my ship."

"Who are you?" Watts asked, then seemed suddenly surprised at his voice. At that point he looked down at his arms and hands and moved them like it was a miracle.

Actually, for Watts' stroke-crippled body, Trans-Galactic Drive and its side effects of regressing a person one year in age with every light year was a miracle.

"I'm Captain Brian Saber," Brian said. "We are about sixty-five light years from Earth on my ship *The Bad Business*.

Watts looked puzzled.

"You know, from the lunch room where we talked about fishing? I'm that Brian."

Again Brian offered his hand and this time Watts took it, leveraging himself out of the sleep coffin and seeming surprised he could stand.

"Your body is regressed sixty-five years," Brian said. "Pretty nifty, huh?"

"But how?" Watts asked, testing out his legs and hands, which actually looked pretty silly with him wearing only his nursing home gown.

"It's a side effect of faster-than-light drive," Brian said. "So they have to use us old people from nursing homes to get out this far. I'll explain it all later. For now, get dressed. There are clothes in the closet there that will fit your young body. I'll be waiting in the next room."

Without giving Watts a chance to answer, Brian spun and left the room, letting the door slide closed behind him.

Brian knew exactly how Watts was feeling.

In a way, he felt it every time he went on a mission.

THREE

AFTER WATTS GOT dressed in standard EPL black pants, vest, tall boots, and loose silk shirt, Brian took him to the dining area next door to Watts' room to get something to drink and so they could sit and talk.

The room had one wall that was a giant window out into space and Brian had to admit, right now the view of the millions of stars and close galaxies was pretty stunning.

The rest of the room was set up at the moment for breakfasts, lunches and dinners at the fake-wood tables. But sometimes, after a major victory, this room was transferred into a party room with a large dance floor for the crew to celebrate and unwind for an evening before going back to their nursing homes. They would be returned within fifteen minutes of leaving, even if they had spent months out in space being young.

Watts had just gone over to the window and stared. Brian gave him the time,

getting himself a soda from a fountain area and sitting at a table to wait.

Ten minutes later Watts just shook his head and came over and sat down.

"This is one hell of a dream," he said.

"Thank heavens for all of us that this is all very real," Brian said.

"Is it really you, Brian?" Watts asked, staring at him.

Brian laughed. "The young version with my old memories."

Then Brian told him about a fishing hole they had talked about in eastern Oregon, and about a stream that Watts used to love to fish in northern Washington.

And then, over the next hour, Brian tried to explain to Watts what was going on, what he knew about that had happened back in the nursing home, and what the EPL wanted of him, from what little the general had said.

"My job is to just show you around and let you get used to all this before the EPL offers you a job," Brian said.

"And if I say no?" Watts asked, smiling.

Brian laughed. "You have to admit, they offer a good benefits package."

At that moment Brian's com link clicked and Marian said, "Captain, we have a problem. Need you on the bridge at once."

Brian stood and told Watts to follow him.

Brian had no idea what kind of problem they might be facing, but Marian sounded very alarmed, or as much as Marian ever got alarmed. She was the calmest person he had ever met under pressure.

As they entered the small bedroom-sized bridge, Brian pointed to an empty chair against the back wall and told Watts to sit there.

In the third chair was Carl Turner, the best navigator Brian had ever had the pleasure to work with.

"Captain," Carl said, glancing up for only a moment as Brian slid into his chair.

Brian instantly knew there was a major problem since Carl normally had a joke or a quip for any moment. No joke meant very serious.

"What's happening," Brian said as he geared up all his heads-up screens.

"Take a look at this on the big screen," Marian said.

In front of all of them a planet showed up with three moons circling it in very fast orbits. That planet must really have a heavy core and gravity well to hold those moons at the speed they were traveling.

"All three of the moons' orbits are exactly five hours Earth Standard," Carl said. "And that planet is in a stable and very, very slow orbit around its sun. In fact, it looks like it's not moving at all."

"Exactly?" Brian asked, staring at the three moons circling what looked to be a desert planet about the same distance from a yellow star as Mars was in their system.

"Exactly," Carl said. "It's what caught my attention."

"Where are we?" Brian asked.

Marian's fingers flew over her panel and the big screen changed to a form of map. A dotted line was damn close to where they were. *The Bad Business* was indicated by a single green light.

The line was the border between the EPL and an alien race that hated the EPL called "The Sticks." They looked like Mantis bugs and had spaceships that were long and narrow.

Brian had not yet had the pleasure to fight them, as this area of the border was known for being very quiet for decades.

Marian brought the map into a tighter focus. The planet was smack on the border and with its slow orbit would be for another two months.

The moons spun from Sticks' space to EPL space and back every five hours.

"Here's a look from our border security monitoring stations of this planetary system," Marian said.

She brought up the image of the strange planet and its three large moons. The image was at an angle and left all three moons blocked from view at one point or another on the EPL side.

"I'm missing the problem," Brian said.

"The system looked strange to me," Carl said. "Never heard of one like it, so I focused our scans in on it and got this."

The big screen showed a close-up of one moon and it seemed to be crawling with long thin bugs.

"They seem to be sending off parts for ships every orbit when the moon is in the monitoring blind spot. The parts, all too small for our sensors, are going toward a nearby planetary system that is behind our monitoring stations."

"Building ships there?" Brian said softly.

"Seems like a slow-moving invasion to me," Marian said.

"Shit, shit, shit," Brian said. He just couldn't believe what he was seeing. This was supposed to be an easy milk-run to show a scientist around and suddenly they had discovered an entire invasion of EPL space.

Brian turned to Marian. "Do they know we are here?"

"I doubt it," Marian said.

"I kept my scans low levels," Carl said.

"Back us out of here about five light years," Brian said. "And find out how long it will take other warships to get manned and with us."

A moment later they flashed into Trans-Galactic drive and then fifteen seconds later dropped out again.

"I'll be go to hell," Watts said from behind them.

Brian glanced around at the guest he had forgotten was even on the bridge. Watts was holding up his left hand and staring at where he had a finger missing.

"Cut that off when I was twenty-nine," Watts said, holding his hand up for Brian to see. "This isn't a dream, is it?"

"At the moment," Brian said, "far from it."

FOUR

THE NEWS FROM the Earth Protection League deep space headquarters wasn't good. A fleet of warships couldn't be with them for three days.

And the order that came back after all the transmissions of data was for *The Bad Business* to slow the Sticks down as much as possible to buy time for a full fleet to get here and engage them.

"Well," Carl said, "That's going to be fun."

"We never planned on living forever, did we?" Marian asked, shaking her head.

Brian turned around to look at Watts. "Sorry, but there's nothing we can do. You are going to have to ride along with us."

Watts shrugged. "From what I understand, I died in the nursing home anyway."

Brian nodded and turned back to Marian. "Put me on ship-wide speaker and give all the crew all the information we have downloaded."

Marian nodded and Brian gave the crew the mission. Then he ended with, "Time to do what they are paying us for."

"We're getting paid?" Carl asked after Brian clicked off.

"Have you looked at that young body in the mirror lately?" Brian said, smiling.

"Every time I come on board," Carl said.

"No wonder you're always the last one to the bridge," Marian said.

"Battle stations, everyone," Brian said to the entire ship before Marian and Carl could get going any more.

He glanced at Carl, "Take us in right over where they are building those warships in our territory."

Carl nodded. "Course in."

"Now."

A moment later they were back in Trans-Galactic flight and then they came out almost over an orbiting construction facility. There were a good ten Stick warships in one stage or another of construction and they were building more construction space docks that looked more like spider webs than the standard space ports that Brian had seen.

"We got them in the early stages," Carl said.

"Gunners, clear this mess out!" Brian said to all his gunners around the ship as

Carl took the ship diving in like a bird at the space docks.

They made five passes at the space docks before there wasn't an alien left alive or a ship in a bigger piece than a dining room table.

They didn't take any return fire at all.

They had gotten lucky with this part.

"Now, let's clear off those moons," Brian said.

"Shields at full power," Marian said.

Again Carl did his magic and they appeared out of Trans-Galactic flight almost over one of the three moons.

"Take it out!" Brian ordered.

The first moon didn't have time to even mount a defense and it took them less than thirty seconds to clear it down to original form with a few new craters as well.

The second moon coming around the planet from the Stick's side of the border was another matter.

"We're taking fire!" Marian said.

"Carl, drop us back a quarter of a light year."

Instantly they were in and out of Trans-Galactic flight again.

"Shields still over ninety percent," Marian said.

"Carl, come in from the border side of that moon if you can."

Instantly they were swooping in again at the moon, only from exactly the other direction as they had been approaching before.

"Take out the guns first," Brian ordered his gunners.

In five minutes, the second moon was in ruins as well.

"Do we break the treaty and go into Sticks' space to clear out that other moon?" Carl asked.

"No," Brian said. "We sit right here, just waiting for it to come around and see what they do now that they know the other two moons and their construction site are destroyed."

"Reporting in to headquarters," Marian said.

"Stay alert everyone," Brian said.

Thirty minutes later Carl and Marian reported that the Sticks on the third moon were abandoning the moon. A Sticks' warship had swung in close and was evacuating the moon.

By the time the moon had crossed into EPL territory, it was empty and Brian and his crew spent less than fifteen minutes destroying what was left.

"Back us a few light years away from the border," Brian said when they were done.

"Thirty of our warships will arrive in three days to help us clear the border of any other attempts at this sort of thing," Marian reported.

"So what do we do between now and then?" Carl asked, grinning.

Brian stood and indicated that Dr. Watts should as well.

"I'm going to try to explain this crazy new world to Dr. Watts," Brian said. "You two hold down the fort and make sure all repairs are under way."

Marian and Carl nodded.

"And tonight," Brian said, smiling, "plan us a party."

"Yes, sir, Captain," Carl said, smiling. "Any special theme?"

"Being alive and young," Brian said.

Dr. Watts just shook his head. "Mind if I drink to that?"

"A lot of us will," Brian said, laughing.

USA TODAY BESTSELLING AUTHOR

DEAN WESLEY SMITH

LAYING THE MUSIC TO REST

A former college professor turned bartender, Doc finds himself trying to save his friends from a ghost under a lake in the wilderness of Idaho.

From diving into a ghost town buried under a lake to trying to stay alive on the sinking deck of the Titanic, this time-travel science fiction novel reads like a roller-coaster ride with all the twists and turns.

First published in paperback in 1989 from Warner Questar Books, Dean Wesley Smith's first published novel gives a lot of hints of his future series and his bestselling career spanning over a hundred and fifty novels.

Published here in its original form, without any changes, just as Dean wrote it almost thirty years ago.

LAYING THE MUSIC TO REST
Part 7

CHAPTER TWELVE

First-Class Stateroom E-7
Second Cycle
April 14, 1912

MARJORIE SAID SHE knew exactly where to start looking.

She led me aft to the rear first-class staircase, a staircase almost as ornate and beautiful as the grand staircase. The stone-tile stairs clicked under our heels and the thick oak railing felt smooth under my hand.

We went down two decks, along a carpeted hall lined with wooden doors, and out onto the second-class promenade on C deck. Twice along the way we had to stop to avoid passengers. The fear of getting shocked had me spooked. From the way Marjorie avoided the passengers, I wasn't the only one. There weren't many passengers out.

The clock over the stairs said it was 11:00 P.M. ship time. Forty minutes until the ship was due to hit the iceberg. I didn't want to think about what I'd do then.

During one of the quick stops, I asked Marjorie what would happen if one of us ran into a passenger head-on. She said she'd only done it once and didn't wake up until cycling. She said it hurt enough that she didn't want it to happen again.

As we stepped outside onto the second-class promenade, the cold hit me like an unexpected punch, knocking the air from me and making it hard to breathe. The wind from the ship's fast pace swirled around the sheltered deck and cut through my shirt. I had been carrying my jacket and swung it around to put it on.

"Don't bother," Marjorie said. She led me to the starboard side and into a foyer with a simple staircase in the center. Even with the door closed behind us, I wanted to put the coat on. I had been too damned cold too many times over the last few days. Instead of getting used to it, I was becoming more sensitive.

I thought Marjorie was going to start down the stairs, but she didn't. We waited to one side until two men came out a wooden door opposite the stairs, then she held the door for me.

This is the library," she said, leading me across the large room filled with stacks of books and assorted tables and padded chairs. "Amazing, isn't it?"

I had to agree. The room was large enough to handle a large city's entire library, building and all. I could see at least two dozen people and the room looked empty. Yet it had a comfortable feel that made me want to stop and browse. I ran my hand along the spines of some of the fine, leather-bound editions. The only thing missing was that it didn't smell like an old, comfortable library. This room had the smell of new books and polished wood. A comfortable smell all by itself.

"You'll end up spending a lot of time in here," Marjorie said. "Only annoying thing is that if you're right in the middle of a book when you cycle, you have to go back to the shelf and get it again. Never have to worry about books getting shelved wrong, though."

"Living here has some wild drawbacks, doesn't it?"

Marjorie gave me a smile as she continued to lead me across the room. "Yes, it does. The one that bothers me the most is that it's senseless to write anything down. It won't be there in six hours. Does wonders for your memory, though."

"I'll bet," I said.

We wound through the books until finally Marjorie said, "Ah, there he is," and headed toward a table occupied by a middle-aged man. She started the introductions while we were still a good ten feet away.

"Craig," Marjorie said, "I'd like you to meet Kellogg Jones. Otherwise known as Doc."

Craig stood and reached out his hand to greet me. "Medical doctor?"

"University," I said, as I shook his hand. His grip felt solid, confident. He stood maybe six foot, had a large beer gut and wore World War II-style navy pants with a pullover sweater. I instantly liked him and had the feeling that he would be someone I'd want on my side, whichever side that may be.

"Craig's the unofficial prisoner historian," Marjorie said. "If anybody would know who you're looking for, he would."

Craig frowned as he sat back down and pointed at chairs for us to join him. "Looking for someone? I know you're new on board. Saw you building the raft last night."

Neither Marjorie nor I moved to accept his offer to sit down. I laughed. "Real new. About nine hours now."

"Thought so," Craig said. "You have that look. Marjorie must have filled you in on how things run around here. Most newcomers are yelling and screaming at about nine hours."

"I'm still giving it some thought."

Craig and Marjorie both laughed. "So tell me," Craig said, leaning back in his chair and putting his hands behind his head, "why are you looking for someone? How could you even know anyone that's here?"

"A very long story," I said.

"Very long," Marjorie joined in. "Too long to go into right now. Do you know of a prisoner by the name of Alex? I vaguely remember the name but can't place it. He's been on board a long time. Seems I remember—"

"There's only one Alex in all the prisoners," Craig said. "He's been here since around the turn of the century. He helped me once with some history about Boston. Short, reddish brown hair. That the guy?"

"Seems like it might be," I said. "I obviously have never met him. You know where we might find him?"

"Sure do," Craig said, looking up across the table at me and smiling. "But I'm real curious as to why you want to find him."

"I got a message from an old friend of his."

"Back real world?" Craig asked.

I nodded.

"For the life of me I can't figure out how you knew he was here."

"Just a hunch, more than anything else," I said. I didn't really want to spend the next hour or more trying to explain my story over again. "Tell you what, after we find him, I'll tell you every little detail. Promise." I gave him my best smile.

"You're not going anywhere, so I suppose I can wait. Toss in some current real-world news and you got yourself a deal."

"With pleasure," I said.

Craig nodded. "Try the first-class reading room. He spends most of his time up there. If he's not over near the windows there, try E-seven."

"Thanks," I said. "One other question. Have there been any other new arrivals the last few days?"

"You mean cycles?" Craig said. "No. Not that I know of. Why?"

"Part of that same big story. If you happen to see a white-haired young woman named Susan, please tell her I'm looking for her?"

Craig nodded, looking very serious. "I sure will. And I'm going to be waiting very impatiently for this story."

"It's a whopper," Marjorie said. "I can promise you that."

We beat a hasty retreat back through the library. "Reading room is right back up where we were," Marjorie said.

"I know," I said. "Saw it the first time around."

We retraced our path, only this time we didn't have to stop for passengers. The halls were almost deserted except for an occasional passenger and a few stewards.

We cut back through the first-class lounge. Only a few men were still there. In one corner, a loud group of seven younger-looking couples were laughing and drinking. One of the women waved at Marjorie as we went by and she waved back.

"They party almost every cycle," she said over her shoulder as she led me toward the bow door of the lounge. "Not much else for us to do."

I didn't like the sound of that one bit. I never was one for parties. Carla always had to drag me to the required university functions and I always managed to drag her out early.

The first-class reading room was deserted and felt cold. Ornately carved wooden tables and padded arm chairs were spaced at comfortable distances around the high-ceilinged room. We walked all the way into the middle of the room and stopped. I felt like I had stumbled into a huge, oversized version of someone's fancy living room that was used only for show. I couldn't imagine how anyone could be comfortable in here.

"Let's try E-seven," I said.

Marjorie glanced over at the old grandfather's clock against the wall. "We're going to have a hell of a time getting there."

"Why?"

"I'll show you." She led me back out into the warm, carpeted hallway and we stood looking out the draped window over the starboard side of A deck. After a moment's wait she pointed toward the bow of the ship.

At first I couldn't see what she was pointing at. Then slowly, out of the dark, a vague, gray shape started to form on the black water, growing in size and heading at the ship. Or I guess I should say the ship was heading at it. It was the iceberg.

As if the world had shifted into a slow-motion silent movie, the ship plowed through the calm sea toward the gray mountain. Finally, when it seemed a direct collision was imminent, the bow of the huge ship slowly moved to the left. The mountain towered above us as the ship slid by the rough wall of ice. I took an unconscious step away from the window. It felt as if the entire side of the iceberg

---

Some Classic Dean Wesley Smith Stories
Available at your favorite booksellers.

was going to come crashing down at any moment. Deep inside the ship I could feel a low rumbling. The drapes beside me shook. Then, just as quickly as it had appeared, the wall of ice was past the ship and receding into the dark.

Except for the constant background hum of the engines, the ship was quiet.

"Going to be passengers everywhere very shortly," Marjorie said. She took me by the arm. "Let's get moving. It might take us a little while to find his room."

I nodded and followed her down the hall toward the grand staircase. My mind felt numb. I had just witnessed the event that had killed over fifteen hundred people. And it had happened so fast, it felt almost like an understatement.

The low, background hum of the engines stopped, leaving the air with a heavy feeling of something missing.

"Heads up," Marjorie said as we started down the right side of the grand staircase. She went to the right and I went to the left rail to get out of the way of two officers running up.

"We have about fifteen minutes before all hell starts breaking loose in the lower halls. We've got to be in some room out of the way before that. Keep an eye out for anyone. They all seem to be in a great hurry and act very erratically."

"Wouldn't you?"

She nodded. "I did."

We made it down to D deck, as far as I had gone the first cycle, before we met anyone else. On D deck we had to move over into the first-class reception area to get out of the way of a dozen passengers. The grand staircase narrowed between D and E decks and we only made it to the landing before we had to retreat in the face of eight passengers all heading upward, laughing as if nothing were wrong.

The next try we only had to dodge one steward.

"This way," Marjorie said and headed through a door and into a wide hall. Closed wooden doors lined the inside of the hall, with electric lamps in the shapes of lanterns on each wall. Twenty-five-foot-long dead-end corridors led off at regular intervals on the outside. Stewards were busy toward the aft end of the long main corridor, knocking politely on doors, starting to wake the occupants. A few of the doors near us stood open as passengers moved into the hall to see what was wrong.

"Got any ideas?" I asked.

"I think lower numbers are usually nearer the front and to the outside. But that pattern doesn't hold for all decks."

"Sounds as good as anything." The floor was starting to tilt noticeably down toward the stern and starboard side. We headed *down* the hall. The first door on the left was E-42. The first door in the nearest side passageway was E-19.

In the next side passageway, the closest two doors were numbered E-17 and E-14.

"We're going the right way," I said as we stopped to let two stewards move quickly past. "About three more side hallways."

"Good," Marjorie said as she watched more passengers file out of the rooms and start for the stairs. "I don't want to be out here much longer."

I agreed with her there. But I also didn't want to be six floors down inside a ship when it sank. Not my idea of giving myself a chance to survive. And I didn't fully believe I was going to end up out on deck again, safe and sound. I knew it had happened once. But I still didn't believe it.

"Here," Marjorie said as she cut down a side passageway and stopped in front of the door labeled E-7.

"Hope someone's home," I said as I knocked on the door.

"Come in," a muffled voice said from inside. "It's open."

"You ready?" Marjorie whispered.

I wasn't sure that something new wouldn't send me screaming back down the hall, but I nodded anyway, and she pushed open the door.

The room was gigantic by a 1990 cruise ship's standards and small by hotel-room standards. A diamond-patterned carpet covered the floor. The walls were half oak paneling and half elaborate wallpaper. A small couch with throw pillows was built into the wall beside the door, and a bed was built into the far wall. Sitting in the room's only chair, his back against the bow wall and his feet up on the edge of the bed, was the same man I had seen in the photograph of Roosevelt, Idaho. He looked up over the edge of the book he was reading and without even a smile said, "May I help you?"

I stood there too stunned to move. My mind wouldn't accept the fact that this was the same man that was standing in front of that tent in that picture, even though he looked like he was, right down to the turn-of-the-century style pants and shirt.

He had a rugged, hard face, accented by a short handlebar mustache. His blue eyes cut at me with a look of annoyance.

Marjorie pushed me far enough into the room to get the door closed behind me. Then she turned and faced the man.

"Alex?" she said.

He nodded, looking first at Marjorie and then back at me, with the same annoyed look.

"My name is Marjorie. This is Kellogg Jones. He's new on board and was looking for you."

"Looking for me?" Alex asked. He got a puzzled frown on his face that cleared his eyes. He stood, closed his book and laid it on the bed. "Do I know you?" He reached out to shake Marjorie's hand, then mine.

I shook my head. "No. But I know of you. And in a fashion I have met Gretchen."

His face seemed to drain of color and he sat down in the chair, his eyes focused on something not in the room. After a moment he came back and looked at me. "That was a long time ago," he said. "Have a seat and tell me about her. There's an extra chair in the room across the hall."

I went across the small side hall and into a matching room. The chair was solid, heavy wood and I ended up dragging it back into Alex's room instead of carrying it.

Marjorie had already sat down on the couch, her legs curled up under her and the pillow behind her back against the wall. I slid the chair over so that we formed a triangle in the small room. I was facing down hill, and if the tilt to the floor got much worse, I wouldn't be able to sit in the chair. I could see why Alex had his chair against the forward wall and his feet up.

"So tell me, Mr. Jones," Alex said, "how you came to meet Gretchen."

"Call me Doc. Everyone else does."

Alex nodded.

I didn't know where to start, so I figured I might as well get the worse part over. "Gretchen is dead."

Alex nodded thoughtfully. "I assumed she would be by now. She must have lived a full life to have met you. I'm glad to hear that."

I looked over at Marjorie and she nodded.

"She died the night you were pulled here," I said.

"But how—" He stared at me with a cold, intense stare. "If this is some sort of joke, I do not find it the slightest bit funny. I was very much in love with Gretchen."

"I'm afraid it's a fact," I said. "Gretchen is the main reason I'm here. She died the night you left. The same night the town of Roosevelt flooded. She has been waiting for you to return."

"Waiting?" All these years?" Again his eyes focused on another place and he had to shake himself to return. "How? How can she be waiting? And what do you mean the town flooded?"

Again I looked over at Marjorie, but she didn't offer help. "She's a ghost."

"A ghost?" he asked. "A spirit? Now I know you are making fun of me. A ghost seems a little farfetched, wouldn't you admit?"

"I didn't believe it either, but I'm afraid it's the truth. She can be clearly seen, and she seems very centered on having you return."

Alex shook his head. "I'm getting very confused."

"I don't blame you," I said. "Let me back up and tell you everything I know. It might make more sense that way."

"A very good idea," he said. He laughed softly. "A very good idea."

I started by telling him about what happened to the town of Roosevelt and what was left of it after eighty years. I told him about Constance and Fred and how Gretchen was hurting them without meaning to. I told him about the dive and about Gretchen playing the piano. Then finally I told him about Susan and how she had come through his grandmother's mirror before I had.

During the entire story, he just nodded, or added a detail about Gretchen or Roosevelt. After I finished, he sat there,

his legs up on the bed, his eyes glazed over in thought.

I couldn't tell if he was accepting my wild story or not. But I was having different troubles. The floor of the cabin was tilting more and more. Halfway through the story I had abandoned the chair and sat down on the carpet. Now I was feeling very trapped. Claustrophobic. I didn't like the idea of being so far inside a ship while it was sinking, even if the two people in front of me were living proof that I would survive it. I would much prefer my chances at swimming.

I looked over at Marjorie. "Think it might be possible to go up and listen to the band?"

She smiled and checked her watch. "Don't think we'd make it."

Alex checked his gold vest-pocket watch. "Just a few more minutes." He looked directly at me, his blue eyes now very clear, even more intense. "Do you think there might be a way back?"

I fought down the fear building in my stomach and tried to give him a straight answer. "I got the impression that Susan thought there was. But we'd have to find her."

"I'd like to help," Alex said. "It's been a long time since Gretchen, but I still have memories of her as if it were yesterday. Before coming here, I would have laughed if you had brought up the possibility of a ghost existing. After eighty-one years on this ship, I tend to believe you."

"Fine," I said. "But couldn't we talk about this up on one of the decks? Doesn't the water come up this high?"

Again Alex checked his watch. "As a matter of fact, it does. Have a look down the hall." He smiled at Marjorie as if they shared some stupid joke.

I opened the door and scampered down the narrow passageway into the very tilted main hallway. No one was in sight. Water swirled one corridor away, rising toward me incredibly fast.

I ran back to Alex's open door. "There's water in the hall. I'm going to try to—"

"Come back inside and close the door," Alex said. His voice was firm and left no room for argument.

I glanced back toward the main hall and then did what he said. Somehow I had to believe this man. If he was wrong, it wouldn't matter much longer. Even if I didn't believe him and tried to make a run for it, it was doubtful that I could make it up those stairs in time.

"Sit here," Alex said, swinging my chair around so that its back rested against the bow bulkhead. "Stick your feet up there." He pointed at the end table beside my chair. Then he sat down and put his feet up on the bed.

I did as I was told. It was like sitting in a chair that had tilted backward and rested against a wall. Only the entire room was tilted, like we were in a carnival fun house. I was not having fun.

"Where we going to meet?" Marjorie asked.

"In heaven, no doubt," I said.

Both laughed.

"How about the first-class lounge?" Marjorie said. "I think Doc just might need another drink."

She was right. I wished I was there having one right now. Water was swirling and bubbling under the door and a wet stain in the carpet was moving across the room lightning fast.

"How deep does it get in here?" I asked, trying to make my grip on the arms of my chair relax before my fingers went completely numb.

"Not very," Alex said as the water started to bubble up under the door like an artesian well.

"Good to hear," I said.

Again they both laughed.

"The first-class lounge would be fine," Alex said. "It will take me a short time to reach it."

"Thirty minutes, then," Marjorie said.

"Don't you think we might want to get started now?" I asked.

Both were laughing at my gallows humor when the room faded and I found myself for the third time in total blackness.

This time, the weight of the backpack felt heavenly against my shoulders and the cold wind felt like my first kiss.

And I was never so glad to see a sunset in my entire life.

CHAPTER THIRTEEN

First-Class Lounge
Third Cycle
April 14, 1912

AS I HAD last time around, I beat Marjorie into the first-class lounge. Only this time I didn't stand and wait for her. I went straight to the bar, watched until the bartender was down the bar and all of the stewards were serving, then jumped in and made myself a drink. Scotch again. My nerves deserved it.

I poured Marjorie a brandy, then went over to the same booth and tried not to gulp my scotch while I took stock of myself and tried to sort out all that had gone on.

First off, I had survived twelve hours of the last six hours of the *Titanic*. I wasn't tired and I wasn't the slightest bit hungry. In fact, I felt full, as if I had just eaten the huge lunch Constance had forced down me. If I got stuck here, that meal was going to do me for years. Constance would be happy to hear that, I was sure.

Not being tired seemed even more amazing, considering that over the last few years I had been getting tired much faster than I used to. If the last twelve hours had been in straight time, I would have been a walking zombie by now. Of course, I had gotten tired a lot because I was bored. The last few days had been anything but boring.

It was fairly obvious that I was in what was called a time loop. But a loop where not everything repeated. In each of my three cycles so far, I had done different things. I wasn't forced to follow the same path. My body started over but my memory didn't. I didn't have the foggiest idea how that could work and the more I tried to figure it out, the more my head ached. Maybe Susan could explain, assuming she was on board and assuming we could find her.

Even if she could explain the time loop, it was going to be one damn long time before I really trusted the cycle to work each and every turn. Just my luck that the one time there was a malfunction I'd be trapped down in a cabin with the water swirling around my toes and a drink in my hand.

"Already fixed yourself a bracer, I see," Alex said as he came up from behind me.

"And one for Marjorie. Didn't know what you were drinking. Want me to make something for you?"

"Thank you, no," he said. "Been pouring my own now for years." He laughed softly to himself as if he'd said something funny, then moved toward the bar.

I watched him as he went behind the bar and worked around the bartender. Alex seemed to know every move the bartender was going to make and was always a fraction of a second ahead when

the guy made it. It didn't seem possible that he was the same Alex who had lived in Roosevelt, Idaho. What had kept him going for eighty years? Why keep living? This was only my third cycle, but I could already tell how life would be if stuck here. And he'd been going around and around for over three hundred cycles.

He ambled back across the lounge, his walk light, almost bouncy on the thick carpet. "You recovered your wits yet?" he asked as he set his drink down on the linen tablecloth and slid into the booth so that he sat facing me.

"Going to take some getting used to."

"I'm afraid you're right about that."

"I imagine you've seen a few over the years."

Again he laughed his soft, easy laugh as he leaned back and twisted his mustache. "That would be an understatement of large proportions. There have been more than I can remember. A large number don't make the transition."

"Transition?"

"They go insane," he said. "Go over the side, kill themselves in some fashion or another. Sometimes they take some of us with them. I'm surprised Marjorie talked to you. Those of us who have been on board a few years have learned to stay clear of the newcomers for a few cycles."

"So that's why no one here has formed a welcoming committee. I was wondering about that during my first cycle."

Alex shrugged. "All of us have helped others at one time or another, as Marjorie obviously helped you. But to my knowledge, nothing organized has ever been done. There is very little organization on any level among the prisoners. We're all stuck here and everything stays the same every six hours. What is there to rule? There's just no need for it."

He looked away into the distance for a moment, then went on. "Except, of course, when incidents occur, such as those murders back a few years." He laughed to himself. "Dreadful episode, that one. We actually had a police force for a short time. It was fun while it lasted."

I was about to ask how murders could be fun when Marjorie came through the stern door to the lounge and waved. I was glad to see her again. I hadn't felt that way about a woman since Carla.

"See you both made it," Marjorie said as she slid into the booth beside me and picked up her drink. "Thanks." She held her drink up and then took a sip. Her smile again made me smile.

She was wearing the exact same thing she had last cycle. So was Alex. It seemed they both had distinct habits they followed. I was learning habits, too. This time I hadn't even bothered to drag the pack over to the wall or put on my coat. Didn't seem to be a need to do either. If one of the other prisoners took something, I'd get it back in six hours.

"Any ideas what we should do next?" Marjorie asked after she took a quick sip of her brandy.

"It seems to me," Alex said, "that finding this Susan should top the list."

"I agree," I said. "But with the size of this ship, that is not going to be an easy task."

"But it is *only* a ship," Alex said. "It would seem logical that since she used my mirror, just as we both did, she is on board somewhere. If that is the case, we will eventually find her or she will find us. We have more than enough time."

"Maybe not," I said.

"Why?" Alex asked, looking directly into my eyes as I'm sure he must have done to witnesses in courtrooms.

"Because we're here," I said. "Someone has gone to a lot of trouble to set this all up and keep us safe and living. Susan said we are all going to be used to start civilization over. My question is, start over after what?"

"Atomic war?" Alex asked.

"How could you know about nuclear war?" I asked.

He laughed. "I've tried to keep up with current news and developments from arrivals. Keep a hand in the real world just in case."

"Makes sense," I said. I took a sip of the smoky-tasting scotch before going on. "Let's stop and logically look at what has happened. First, Susan knew what the mirror was. Second, she wanted to go through it for who knows what reason. Third, she said others would want to use the mirror. Fourth, we are here and cycling around on top of ourselves every six hours. Over the years has anyone on board come up with a reason for all of this?"

Alex shook his head. "None that would hold water," he said. Again he laughed softly at some private joke. I watched him for a moment. I suppose I would laugh a lot after eighty years on a ship. Assuming that I had any sanity left at all.

"Then it might follow," I said, "that no matter how much we don't like the idea, our civilization might come to an abrupt end real soon. Someone set up whatever device it took to guarantee—"

I stopped and smiled at them. It had suddenly occurred to me that I knew exactly where Susan was.

"What's wrong?" Marjorie asked.

"I think I've solved the problem of finding Susan," I said. "She said the mirrors were only triggers and focuses. She said that the real time mechanism would be at the other end. This end. Alex, do you know of anywhere on the ship that seems to be off limits to prisoners? Or that seems in the slightest big different?"

"I see what you're getting at," Alex aid. "The main device would be somewhere on board and Susan would go to it. Very logical thinking. You would make a good member of the bar. But I'm afraid I know of no place on the ship that would even remotely fit your conclusion."

"How about the center?" Marjorie asked. "Wouldn't it be in the center of the ship?"

"Possibly," I said. "But not necessarily. However, it might be in the middle of where everyone cycles. I come out forward on the boat deck. Marjorie, you said you were down below somewhere?"

"Down on E deck on the port side and slightly to the rear."

"I cycle onto E deck, also," Alex said. "Just forward of my cabin."

"Seems that if we got enough places spotted," I said, "we might be able to narrow down this search to an area on a couple of decks."

"Craig has that kind of information," Marjorie said. "It's his hobby. I know he asked me all sorts of questions like that once."

"And he asked me, also," Alex said. "He knows where the plans of the ship's decks are located. But I must say I am hesitant about imparting any of your information to fellow prisoners."

"Why?" Marjorie asked.

I could see why. The same reason I felt hesitant about telling Craig. "We're looking for the way back to the real world. We don't want to get the others' hopes up too soon."

"As well as have them interfere," Alex said.

"Very good point," I said. "Can this Craig be trusted?"

"He seems to be the one most of the prisoners turn to when something needs to be done." Marjorie said. "I guess you could say he is the unofficial leader. He doesn't push it, though. And no one runs against him."

"He can be trusted," Alex said. His voice was flat and serious.

"Well then," I said. "How about someone fixing us all more drinks and we'll go tell the man a story."

"I'll get the drinks," Marjorie said, downing the last of hers and standing. "Alex?"

"Brandy," Alex said. "Porter's, down on the shelf to the right." He laughed softly to himself as we followed Marjorie over to the bar.

I figured that as much as he laughed, there must be a running comic monologue going on inside his head. I didn't want to think about what I'd be like after eighty years on the same ship. I doubted if I would be in half as good shape as he was. I'd probably laugh more to keep from crying.

Now Available
from all your favorite booksellers in trade paper and electronic editions.

Marjorie slid our drinks to us across the oak bar and we headed out the aft door of the lounge in the direction of the second-class library.

"That's pretty wild, all right," Craig said after I had finished telling the basic part of my story for the third time in the last eight hours. I was getting it down real pat. A little more practice and I could take the entire show on the road.

"I warned you," Marjorie said. She'd heard the story the same three times and seemed to be believing it more each time.

We had found Craig sitting alone at the same table in the library he'd been at the previous cycle. Again, as we had worked our way toward his table, I had an overwhelming desire to run my hands along the leather books and take deep breaths of the air that smelled of new shelves and new books. So I had done it. Alex had laughed and followed my example. I was beginning to really like Alex.

Marjorie had sat down next to Craig. Alex and I had sat down across the oak table from him. It had taken me about fifteen minutes to tell him the bare-bones outline of my last few days. I hadn't mentioned the part about the world possibly coming to an end. That was one factor I still didn't want to believe myself.

During the entire time, Craig sat with his hands on the smooth table, leaning forward, listening to me. I knew from his eyes that he wasn't missing a thing. Now that I was finished he was going to fill in some holes with questions. "Does this ghost called Gretchen sound right to you?" Craig asked Alex.

Alex nodded. "I'm afraid it does. I did get pulled here as Gretchen rejected my offer of marriage. I've always wondered why she did that."

"She didn't think she was worthy of you," I said, repeating what Steven had found out.

"She didn't?" Marjorie asked.

Alex nodded. "I knew of her fear. I hoped to talk her past it." His eyes seemed to be looking back into another world as he said, "I was not allowed the time."

Craig nodded and turned to me. "I don't understand why you purposely triggered the mirror. Seems like a stupid thing to do to me. No offense."

"It was," I said. "But I had my reasons. Partly to help my friends. I came to take this man back to what's left of the town of Roosevelt." I patted Alex on the shoulder.

Craig laughed a hearty, full laugh. "If you figure out how to do that, please tell the rest of us."

"That's why we came to see you," Marjorie said.

Craig looked at her and then at me, his eyes again intense and very serious. "You have a way?"

"Not yet," I said. "But I think Susan does. We need to find her. But we need to do it quietly. There seems to be no need in getting up the hopes of everyone over what may well turn out to be a wild idea."

Craig nodded. "I agree. But what makes you think this woman knows any more about all this than anyone else?"

I quickly sketched in what Susan had said about this being a reseed group for after worldwide destruction. And I told him what she had said about the main transmitter for all the mirror triggers being here at this end. As I told him that, I saw his eyes take on the look of comprehension.

"Okay," he said. "You obviously have an idea where this device may be. Right? And you're assuming she is there. Right?"

"Exactly," I said. "We were hoping that you might be able to help us pinpoint where people cycle to each time. We think the device might be in the center."

"Makes sense," Craig said. He glanced at his watch. "The plans for the ship are up in the officers' quarters on the boat deck. We've got about an hour before too many officers fill those rooms. I could mark on the plans where everyone I can remember cycles to. I think I can remember most everyone. And even a few who are no longer with us."

"I don't think we need to be that precise. How about doing a rough outline of each deck and marking generally where everyone appears? If there's going to be a pattern, we should be able to tell from that."

Craig nodded, slid his chair back, and stood. "I'll get some paper."

Over the next two hours, Craig proceeded to amaze me with his clear thinking and his fantastic memory for details. He sketched each deck, starting with the boat deck and working downward. He used the grand staircase as his main reference points. For each person, he drew a small circle, stating their name out loud and putting their initials inside the small circle. He remembered hundreds of people's locations. And on four people that he couldn't remember, he knew where they were and sent Marjorie and Alex off to ask them.

My circle on the starboard side, front section of the boat deck was the last circle he put in place.

The pattern was very clear. The seven top decks had circles. The boat deck had six, spaced uniformly around the entire deck and F deck had five, also scattered throughout the deck.

About twenty circles dotted both A deck and E deck. Thirty circles filled both B and D decks, scattered more toward the bow and aft of the ship, with none in the direct center area of either drawing. On C deck, twenty circles dotted both ends of the ship, with not one circle filling the middle.

I kept staring at the large open area in the middle of C deck. It was as if there was a giant hole right in the middle of the ship. It seemed very obvious that whatever device ran the mirrors was somewhere near the center of that hole. Susan probably had had the equipment to find it. We were just going to have to search.

Craig drew a large circle in the center of C deck. "That's on this same deck," he said. "Let's narrow this way down and only deal with the very small center section and forget the rooms along both sides, as well as the areas anywhere near the two staircases. All right?"

I nodded and he went on.

"In the center section between the two boiler casings there are three crosscorridors that run from the port hall to the starboard hall, a distance of over sixty feet." He quickly sketched in the details on his drawing.

"There are maybe thirty first-class rooms in that area, to my knowledge all occupied by passengers. There are also steward service areas and a half dozen small shops."

"What is in the very center corridor?" I asked.

"Only rooms," Alex said. "Four large suites on each side of the corridor.

"Shall we go take a look?" Craig said, and started to stand.

"Caution," Alex said, "would be prudent in this situation."

"I agree," I said. My sixth sense was screaming for us to be careful. I didn't know exactly why. Something about the way Susan had said others would want to use the mirror. I agreed with Alex. We needed to be very careful.

"Why?" Craig asked, seating himself after it became obvious that none of the rest of us were ready to run off and search just yet.

"It would seem logical," Alex said, "that the people who arranged to have us all here also arranged to have their device protected."

"That's a good point," I said. "But there may be more to it than that. Susan mentioned that her goal was to protect this or any seed group from another seed group. And at some point she mentioned one of the groups was called Lomax. I think I was starting to laugh at the moment she was telling me, so I didn't ask any questions. Wish I had now. But you can imagine how farfetched this all sounded sitting beside a lake in the Idaho wilderness. However, she did say that these Lomax are biologically altered in some fashion."

Craig snorted his disbelief. "Are you kidding? Just how would they do that?"

I shrugged. "I don't know how whoever does this does this." I waved at the library around us. "I'd only read about time travel and ghosts in novels up until three days ago. I have a much greater acceptance of the possibility of biologically altered people than I do of sitting on the *Titanic*."

Craig laughed.

"When did you get here?" I asked.

"In 1941. Why?"

"Over the last few years, there have been what was called test-tube babies. Babies that were started in labs and then implanted in women. In 1990, that is an accepted medical fact."

Craig shook his head. "You'd think after being in this craziness all these years, I would be more open-minded. All right. What do you suggest we do?

Marjorie glanced at her watch. "We've only got about twenty minutes."

My stomach clenched up like she'd hit me with a solid right hook. No matter what we found, there was no way I was going to be anywhere but out on a deck when this ship started to go down. I didn't care how cold I would get. There would be no sitting in a cabin with water running around my feet this time.

"My suggestion," Alex said, "would be that we stroll in pairs through the area, noting any circumstance that might seem out of the ordinary."

Craig nodded. "Let's meet in the grand staircase area. Alex and I will go together and take the starboard side. You and Marjorie take port side. All right?"

Marjorie and I waited a full minute after Craig and Alex had left the second-class stairway's foyer before we crossed the cold promenade to the starboard door.

We didn't say anything, but as we passed the first-class stairway, she took my arm. I could feel the tension in her grip. She must have walked these same halls hundreds of times, yet now she seemed afraid. I was too, and damned if I could figure out why. Amazing how I could create fear where none had existed and not really feel fear when I should have been running like hell.

Just before the first crosscorridor, we had to move out of the way of a steward pushing a small cart. Other than him, the entire port-side hall, a football field long, was completely empty. The brown carpet was soft and the wood panels were again oak. Chandelier-style lights hung like streetlamps every fifteen feet. Walking down that hall was like drifting through a nightmare. And I felt lost and very much out in the open.

The first crosscorridor was also empty. All the doors were closed.

However, one woman occupied the center cross passageway. She was standing with her back against the aft wall, facing stateroom C-85. She had short black hair, wore a pair of brown pants and a windbreaker-type jacket. She stood in a parade-rest military position, hands behind her back.

I guessed her to be barely over five feet tall, with very powerful shoulders and an even more powerful-looking pistol-like device strapped to a wide belt around her hip.

As we walked by, she turned to look at us. I had the feeling she was looking right through me, as if I were nothing more than a piece of furniture. She turned back to staring straight ahead before we passed the hall. We were of no importance and no threat to her.

Marjorie and I walked the rest of the length of the hall in silence, her grip firmly on my arm. It was clear I had seen a second traveler from the future. Whether this woman was a Lomax or not, I didn't know. For some reason I had pictured biologically altered people as being huge, lumbering giants, stomping around scaring us little people. I suppose that was the fault of too many grade-B movies. But just maybe they were and the guard woman was one of Susan's people. Hell, I didn't know and I could think of no good way of finding out. I didn't like that thought one bit.

A few moments later, there was a rumbling deep down inside the ship as the *Titanic* struck the iceberg.

I liked that even less.

To be continued…

~

USA *Today* Bestselling Writer

DEAN WESLEY SMITH

A STUDY OF AN ACCIDENT

A Bryant Street Story

Dan remembers clearly the time before the accident.

He remembers his wonderful wife and daughter. Impossible to forget. He refuses to eat or work or even move most days.

He made a mistake, they died. He lives. He blames himself for their deaths.

Someone knocks on his home door. And the truth flips as only it can on Bryant Street.

A STUDY OF AN ACCIDENT
A Bryant Street Story

ONE

THE BLINDS OF the living room had been closed for six months, and only two light bulbs still worked, giving the room a constant feel of depressive gloom. Deep black shadows extended from the once-modern furniture, extending across the oak-colored hardwood floors like stains.

The room smelled of rotted food, a foul odor that now seemed to have gotten coated onto everything.

The television flickered, casting its own light and then dark shadows around the room as scene after scene of meaningless programs and ads ran past.

Six months ago, this house had been alive, a bright place to live and raise a family.

Dan and Jennifer and ten-year-old Denise had all been happy together.

Sitting in his chair in the dark living room facing the mindless television, Dan could imagine he sometimes still heard the happy laughter of Denise as she played in her room down the hall or helped Jennifer with dinner or a project.

Denise, with her bright smile, blue eyes, and long blonde hair used to light up a room wherever she went. Her mother, Jennifer, had been the same way.

And often the three of them would watch a movie together, Dan in his chair, Jennifer and Denise on the couch, a bowl of popcorn between them.

He had loved those movie nights.

Magic nights he would tell Jennifer later, after Denise was off in her room.

And Jennifer had always agreed.

Now the house was dead.

He might as well be.

It had been an accident.

TWO

THE DAY OF the accident started like any normal Tuesday. He kissed Jennifer goodbye in their kitchen and then gave Denise a squeeze and a kiss.

He got into his BMW to head to his office in the McClaskel building. He worked there as a corporate attorney, specializing in property acquisitions.

He liked his job, actually. Found it interesting and challenging and rewarding since he and Jennifer never really were short of money.

He also liked his new car and the new-car smell of the leather. He splurged and got himself a new BMW every year, mostly because he could.

His office was a corner office on the sixteenth floor looking over the downtown area of the city. He had two large

plants that framed the windows and a large mahogany desk, plus a couch and chair tucked against one wall with a mahogany coffee table in front of them.

It was a beautiful office.

He hadn't returned to it since the accident.

They were holding his job for him, but he wasn't sure if he could ever return.

On the day of the accident, everything had gone normally. He had had lunch with two of the other lawyers and three assistants in a nearby pub. He even had a glass of freshly brewed ale. He remembered it tasting smooth and rich and he planned on returning the next day for another glass.

He wasn't much of a drinker, but he enjoyed a good ale.

Back in the office after lunch, he had worked on two cases, one right after another and by three p.m. he had finished up both.

That was when Anna from accounting came in and asked him for some of his time to figure out a few things about a third case. She had an accounting puzzle she needed his help with.

Now Dan had flirted with Anna a few times, but all innocently. He had never fooled around on Jennifer and had no thoughts of doing so.

He loved his wife and his daughter more than anything in the world.

Anna was about his age of thirty-five, had long blonde hair, and large green eyes. She also had a bright sense of humor and a body that looked like it was out of a swimsuit issue of *Sports Illustrated*.

He had heard she was divorced with no kids and was enjoying her freedom, but he didn't ask her about any of that.

The day of the accident, Anna had on a white blouse that showed hints of a lacy bra under it. She had on a business skirt and had her hair pulled back and tied.

For over an hour, they sat on his couch, side-by-side, going over the accounting ledgers she had brought on the coffee table. They joked and laughed and he enjoyed the company and the challenge of finding what they were looking for.

By 4 p.m. they had finished and were both sitting on the couch sipping on bottles of water, just talking.

And then something happened that surprised Dan and made him feel really powerful at the same time.

Anna leaned over and kissed him.

Her kiss was very different from Jennifer's tentative butterfly kiss. And as Anna kissed him, she pressed into him and he responded, kissing her back.

And the next thing he knew, he had tipped over on the couch and she was on top of him.

They were both still dressed when the first part of the accident happened.

"Daddy! Look what I bought!"

His office door opened and in walked Jennifer and Denise, both smiling until they saw the scene on the couch.

They both stopped and stared.

Anna scrambled to her feet, grabbed the accounting ledgers from the coffee table and fled while Dan just stood there.

He didn't know what to say to either his wife or his young daughter.

What could he say?

After a moment, Jennifer had said to him in her cold, angry voice, "We need to talk when you get home."

He had nodded.

Jennifer took Denise's hand and they turned and left without another word.

That was the last time he had seen them.

By the time he had managed to collect himself to go home and explain to Jennifer what had happened, the second part of the accident had happened and his wife and daughter were both gone.

Dead.

Fifteen minutes after leaving his office, Jennifer had drifted into the oncoming lane of traffic and was hit by a large semi-truck.

Both Jennifer and Denise were killed on impact.

Dan knew he had killed them because Jennifer must have been crying while driving and she had never been that good a driver as it was.

He had no memory of the funeral.

He had little memory of the last six months sitting in his dark empty house.

He was as good as dead as well.

He just hadn't stopped breathing yet.

THREE

AT SOME POINT on some day around six months after the accident, there was a pounding on the door.

Dan assumed it was in the middle of the afternoon because of the program flickering in front of him. But he wouldn't have bet on even that much.

"Go away," he shouted from his chair. "I'm not buying."

"It's Detective Carson," a man's voice shouted back. "I need to talk with you."

Dan just shook his head, clicked off the television, and climbed to his feet. He had on jeans that hadn't been washed in any recent memory and an old work shirt he had put on a few days ago as one of his last clean shirts left.

He went to the front door and opened it, letting in the bright light that made his eyes hurt for a moment. Clearly it was a nice day outside.

The quiet suburban street he lived on seemed extra quiet at the moment. Only a black sedan seemed out of place along the green grass and flowerbeds that lined the street.

A heavy-set man stood at the door holding his gold badge. "I'm Detective Carson. We have the results of the cause of your wife's accident."

Dan just shook his head and stepped out on the porch to talk with the detective.

Carson had a strong grip and seemed to give off an air of control. He was fairly short and had a large beer-gut pushing out his suit coat.

"They are dead," Dan said. "Car accident ruled Jennifer's fault. Why investigate?"

"We have to do a complete investigation on all fatal accidents to determine the exact cause."

"And did you?" Dan asked, not really wanting to be a part of this conversation.

"The cause of your wife and daughter's death was because she was distracted while driving," Carson said.

Dan knew that.

He knew he had been at fault. He didn't need to have some detective tell him that.

Dan knew that he had killed his wife and daughter.

Then Detective Carson said, "She was texting."

That shocked Dan to his core.

He blinked twice and looked at the detective, who was just staring at him.

"Texting?" Dan asked, making sure what he had heard was correct.

The detective nodded. "Were you and your wife having marriage issues?"

Dan opened his mouth, then closed it. Then managed to ask, "Why?"

"This is her final text," Carson said. He opened a green file he had been holding under his arm and handed Dan a sheet of paper.

The words made no sense at first and it took Dan twice reading them before he actually understood what they said.

I am free!!! Caught bastard with your friend. Divorce to follow.

There was a response.

"Wonderful! We can finally be together. I knew Anna would come through!"

When Dan looked up from the page, Detective Carson said, "She was texting her response when she drifted in front of the truck. Do you know who she was texting?"

"Do you?" Dan asked, reading the words one more time and trying to get them to sink in.

He had been set up. Jennifer had wanted to leave him. But because of Denise, she couldn't. So Jennifer had set him up with Anna.

There would have been no way after that for him to argue against a divorce.

"I do," Detective Carson said. "Do you know a Susan Fields?"

"Jennifer's best friend," Dan said.

Dan remembered her standing off to one side at the funeral, crying. She was being comforted by another woman and an older man. Dan hadn't been up for talking with her.

"Very, very best friend," Carson said. "We dug up evidence that Jennifer and Susan had been having an affair for years. Since right after your daughter was born, it seems."

"Oh," Dan said, more stunned than he had felt since hearing the news of Jennifer and Denise's deaths.

Jennifer was gay and having an affair.

None of that made any sense at all in the wonderful life the three of them seemed to have had.

"You didn't know, did you?" Carson asked.

Dan shook his head.

"I didn't think so," Carson said.

"Does Susan know she was the one that killed Jennifer and Denise?" Dan asked.

"She did," Carson said, nodding. "She overdosed a month after the accident."

"Oh," was all Dan could say to that as well. Susan wasn't even around to be angry at and blame.

But Susan had had more courage than he had had over the last six months. He had just wallowed in self-pity; she had acted on her grief.

"Here is a copy of the file on everything we discovered in the investigation," Detective Carson said. "I figured you needed to know."

Carson handed him the thin file.

"Thank you," Dan said.

"There is one more thing I think you need to know as well," Carson said, standing there, looking like he might jump and run. He didn't look happy at all telling Dan all this and Dan didn't blame him in the slightest.

"Worse than this?" Dan asked, holding up the file.

Carson nodded. "The information is in there, but figured it was better to hear it coming from me than just read it."

"Go ahead," Dan said.

"Denise was not your biological daughter," Carson said. "We did mandatory DNA matching after the accident and discovered that fact fairly quickly. We have no idea who the father might have been."

Dan nodded, holding onto the folder like it was about to burn him.

Actually, the news in it had already burned him.

And oddly enough, the same news gave him a flickering flame of life again.

"Thank you, Detective," Dan said. "I mean that."

"If you need my help on anything," Carson said, "feel free to call."

Dan nodded and stood in the sun on his front porch, holding the folder with his past and his future in it as Detective Carson walked back to his black sedan parked at the curb.

Then Dan turned and went back into the darkness of his home.

In one conversation, it had become his home now.

Not the burial chamber for every member of a supposedly happy family.

Jennifer had wanted to leave this house and take Denise.

And she must have known that Denise was not his child.

Dan wondered when she was going to tell him that bit of news. More than likely after a lot of years of child support.

But that didn't matter. He would have always thought of Denise as his daughter, no matter what.

Jennifer and her lover Susan had taken Denise from him.

He would never forgive either of them for that.

Ever.

He put the folder in his chair and went to the blinds and opened them on all the front windows.

And then he opened the windows as well, letting in the fresh air of a new day.

There was a lot of smell to get out of this house.

Smell of stale food and dirty laundry.

Smell of six months of self-pity.

And the smell of years of betrayal.

But the bright light of the truth and a few open windows to a future might just be what was needed.

~

USA Today **Bestselling Writer**

DEAN WESLEY
SMITH

DREAMING LARGE
A Seeders Universe Story

The Dreaming Large, a Seeders mother ship vanishes without a trace while approaching the edge of a galaxy.

Chairman West and his crew on the Rescue One *must find out what happened to the huge mother ship. And the over half-million lives on it.*

But as they approach the galaxy's edge, the last known position of the big moon-sized mother ship, what they find surprises them all.

They find nothing. Absolutely nothing.

A galaxy-spanning science fiction story of the unknowns in space.

DREAMING LARGE
A Seeders Universe Story

ONE

THE LAST THREE years had gone faster than Chairman Evan West had expected. Around him on the bridge of the *Rescue One*, the fifteen members of his main crew were all standing ready at their stations on the three levels, all scanning ahead as much as they could.

He knew that through the entire ship the thirty thousand people on board were also watching intently.

West was a tall, thin man with bright green eyes, balding head, and wide shoulders. People said he had a smile that made him a lot of friends and he liked to laugh and have fun.

Lately he hadn't smiled much.

The air was tense in the large room around him, but professional. The large screen that filled the tall wall in front of them only showed the quickly approaching front edge of the small galaxy they were calling Destination. The galaxy had a number, but no one called it by that anymore.

West stood beside his large chairman's chair, watching not only his instruments, but those of his second and third in command at their stations on either side of him.

Nothing.

Just nothing out of the ordinary at all.

They were on a mission to find out what had happened to the *Dreaming Large*, one of the huge Seeder mother ships. It had vanished in the small galaxy they were now approaching.

That had been four years ago, a short time for a Seeder, but a very long time for a major mother ship to vanish completely.

Mother ships were the size of large moons and could hold a thousand ships and upwards of a half million people. It was from the mother ships that Seeders spread humanity from one galaxy to another, always moving forward.

Chairman West had been a seeder now for three thousand years and had seen many galaxies along the way. And he had helped in birthing more billions of human societies than he wanted to even try to imagine.

He loved his job.

He didn't much like this mission. His wife and best friend, Tammy, had been on the *Dreaming Large* when it vanished. He missed their nightly routines of telling each other their days through trans-warp link, even when they had been apart for years. He loved her and always had loved her. And he missed her now more than he wanted to ever admit.

Their plan had been for him to finish up the last part of a seeding mission in the previous galaxy and then his ship and a dozen other front-line ships with him would catch up with the *Dreaming Large*. He liked working the front edge of the seeding as he always did after the terraforming was finished.

He had worried for the three years it took them at full trans-warp speed to get here and he had missed Tammy every moment of it. He had no idea what they were going to find. No one had an idea, even though the speculation was rampant.

How could a major Seeder mother ship simply vanish?

Without a word of notice, the two chairmen who jointly ran the mother ship had stopped reporting in to Chairman Ward and the other overseeing body of the Seeders.

When that had happened, Chairman Ward had contacted him and the idea of *Rescue One* was born.

There were twenty-two mother ships now, built over centuries, with more being built all the time. The *Dreaming Large* was the first to have vanished.

Tammy had been one of the head botanists on *Dreaming Large*. She had loved her job, just as he loved his.

The *Rescue One* had been built specialty for this mission. Unlike most Seeder's ships, the *Rescue One* had a full military contingent and four warships on board, commanded by West's best friend, Admiral Cline. Seeders, by their very mission and scouting ahead, never had much need for military until some of the growing new human cultures hit their early space age stage. So to even put together a military fleet, Cline had scrounged through some more advanced human cultures recently seeded for ships and enough new Seeders to man the ships.

It had taken Cline as long to put his force together as it had to build the *Rescue One*.

The *Rescue One* had been built in preparation for almost anything they might find. It also had in its huge hanger twenty of the Seeder's fastest scout ships, all crewed and ready to go.

And it had room, if necessary, for upwards of a hundred thousand survivors, a fraction of the humans who had been on the *Dreaming Large* when it vanished.

Now, finally, after the year of building and three years of travel at the fastest trans-warp speeds any seeder ship could go, they were almost there.

"Anything?" West asked, breaking the silence on the large bridge and glancing around the three levels at his bridge crew.

All of them just shook their heads.

"Full stop at scouting distance from the edge of Destination," he ordered.

"We'll be at full stop in one minute," Korgan said.

Korgan was his second in command and had been chairman of his own scout ship before volunteering to go on this mission. He had family, a son and a daughter, on the *Dreaming Large*.

In fact, a good third of the crew of the *Rescue One* had family or some personal connection to crew on the *Dreaming Large*.

That made this crew very, very motivated to find the lost mother ship.

"Dropping out of trans-warp now," Korgan said, his voice seeming to almost echo in the silence of the large bridge.

"Full scans," West said.

Then he motioned to Korgan to have the crews of the scout ships stand ready and be scanning as well.

West moved over and stood beside his chair. He couldn't make himself sit in the chair until they knew what had happened to *Dreaming Large*. But from where he stood, he could see all the data streaming in.

It was a small spiral galaxy on the scheme of things, with about 80 billion stars of all standard sizes. It showed no unusual areas at all.

And not a sign of the *Dreaming Large*. Nothing.

The huge mother ship had just vanished.

TWO

WEST GOT UP from his chairman's chair after a few minutes and walked slowly around to all the stations on his bridge, not so much for information, but to give everyone some time and let himself relax a little.

He had been preparing for this moment for four years. Rushing anything now might lead to even more problems.

Finally, after the longest half hour he had ever spent on the bridge, he broke the intense silence.

"Let's have some reports," he said. "So everyone can be together on this. And broadcast these reports to the entire ship please."

Korgan nodded for West to go ahead.

"Anything unusual at all about Destination?"

Three stations reported in that there was nothing unusual. Then Korgan added. "What we are reading matches exactly the last reports of the scout ships two hundred years before the *Dreaming Large* arrived here."

West nodded. "Any signs of alien or human habitation?"

Six reports came in quickly, one after another, cutting the small galaxy down into six quadrants, just as it would have been seeded.

Nothing.

No alien life, no human life, no remains of any ship anywhere.

As with most galaxies, this one was empty. And if it had an alien race at any level anywhere in the galaxy, the entire galaxy would have just been left alone and the *Dreaming Large* would have gone on to the next empty galaxy.

Not one sign that the *Dreaming Large* had even started terraforming the Goldilocks zone planets around yellow stars. Whatever had happened, it had happened before the *Dreaming Large* entered Destination.

"More information as we have it," West said, signaling to Korgan to cut the communication to the entire ship.

West did one more walk around the bridge, looking at details on a few reports, but finding nothing different at all.

Finally, he went down to stand near his station.

"Rescue One," he said, "please put on the screen a two dimensional representation of the galaxies closest to Destination. Limit the galaxies to a one year travel time for the *Dreaming Large* from this point."

Thirty-one galaxies came up, represented as dots. There were a couple clusters and ten galaxies seemed to have formed a group. Over the last three years he had stared at this very map more than he wanted to admit.

But he knew that the *Dreaming Large* would not have gone to any of those other galaxies without reporting in. And with Destination being an empty galaxy, perfect for seeding, there would have been no reason to move on.

This was exactly what he had feared. What Chairman Ward had also feared.

"Now, *Rescue One,*" West said to his ship, "please add into the scanning equipment the ability to see pockets of empty space."

Everyone on the bridge crew just stopped and looked at him like he had lost a marble or two.

Almost no one had heard of empty space. He hadn't either until this mission started.

West had been briefed by Chairman Ward on the very reality of empty space, or void space as it was sometimes called.

Basically, empty space was a very small bubble in space, often not more than the size of a standard solar system, where space was completely empty and time and the rules of physics did not apply for some reason inside it.

Over the centuries, Seeder ships had just vanished when they ran into a bubble of empty space.

And they would often emerge thousands, if not hundreds of thousands of years later having only spent less than a ship-board few hours in empty space.

Chairman Ward had warned West that if there were no logical reasons for *Dreaming Large* to have vanished, no signs of any debris, or any human survivors, then West was to look for empty space pockets.

The scientists on some of the more advanced Seeder ships had developed a program to show complete emptiness, something normal space did not have.

It had taken the scientists three years of frantic work to finally develop and test the long-range scanning program.

And if this worked, every Seeder ship would get the program as an update and hopefully no more ships would be lost to centuries in an empty space bubble.

For the year that the scanning program had been uploaded to *Rescue One,* the scientists had continued to make adjustments and sent them along. West had told no one about any of it.

"Loaded," *Rescue One* said.

"Display on the screen as dots the empty space areas within four galaxies radius of this location," West said.

Then red dots appeared. Only about eight total in that much space, but one was seemingly right where they were.

They were within brushing distance of the edge of an empty space bubble.

"Shit!' West said. "Back us away from the edge of that thing to a distance of two light years."

West couldn't believe that they had almost vanished right into empty space as well.

That had been far, far too close.

"We're back away from it," Korgan reported. "What exactly is empty space?"

"That's where the *Dreaming Large* is trapped," West said.

The big mother ship was right here very close to them, only stuck in a bubble of no time and space. And the mother ship might not emerge for a hundred thousand years.

All West could see in his mind was the smiling face of his wife.

Somehow, they had to rescue the big ship, even though, more than likely, no one on the big ship even knew anything was wrong yet.

But they had to do it.

Somehow.

THREE

OVER THE NEXT five years, the *Rescue One* went from a military-based rescue operation to a full-fledged science ship. West had remained as Chairman on request, a request that Chairman Ward had gladly granted.

And Chairman Ward had put West in charge of the overall mission. All ship's chairmen reported to him.

Entire parts of *Rescue One* were being reconfigured into research labs to study the empty space bubble holding the *Dreaming Large* mother ship.

Admiral Cline had taken all his military ships and headed back to help out at the last seeded galaxy with upcoming wars between developing human planets.

The fleet of scout ships they had brought with them all scattered out to do what they do, scout ahead, map galaxies and spot trouble galaxies that had the occasional growing alien race.

Almost every day another science ship arrived at *Rescue One* and took a location either in space near *Rescue One* or on one of the large decks where the military ships and scout ships had once been housed.

Almost fifty smaller science ships had now surrounded the small bubble of empty space, studying it, trying to see inside it.

Every Seeder's ship now had the scanning ability to see and avoid empty space bubbles, something that West had no doubt would save ships from losing thousands and thousands of years.

Now they just had to figure out a way to get the *Dreaming Large* out of there in under a few thousand years.

Every day Chairman West had a meeting with the four top science advisors to get reports on any progress. They usually met for breakfast in his own kitchen in his apartment, taking turns cooking and cleaning and talking about the problem.

All four were Chairman of their own major science ships.

It was right before one meeting, about six months after they had figured out where *Dreaming Large* was, that West came up with an idea. He had been sitting at his kitchen counter, staring at a surface rendering of the patterns on the border of the empty space and he suddenly saw it a different way.

They had been working to find a way to shield themselves from the effects of the empty space, go in and shield *Dreaming Large* as well. What would happen if they just drained the empty space out into normal space?

Or better yet, filled empty space with normal space.

In essence, they needed to pop the bubble, leaving the *Dreaming Large* surprised at all the company it suddenly had around it.

The four scientists loved that idea and after the meeting, West contacted Chairman Ward and told him about it to get scientists in numbers of galaxies working on the problem as well.

It took seven more years to find the solution.

Seven very long and frustrating years.

Now West stood on the bridge of the *Rescue One* yet again, sixteen years after he had agreed to join this project, ready to try to finally release *Dreaming Large*.

As everyone had been warned, no one on *Dreaming Large* would even realize they had been in trouble. As far as those on board the giant mother ship knew, only a few seconds had transpired since they entered empty space and their trans-warp drives had suddenly shut down.

If what *Rescue One* and all the other ships were about to do worked, the hundreds and hundreds of ships that now swarmed the area would suddenly just appear to those on *Dreaming Large*.

If it worked.

And if the forces didn't pull *Dreaming Large* apart.

Chairman Ward and others had said that the giant mother ships were designed to withstand plowing into planets and going right on through. Ward wasn't worried about that at all.

But West was.

They had calculated the trajectory where *Dreaming Large* had entered the empty space bubble and cleared every ship out of the way where it would be headed.

What they were going to try to do was in essence take the pressure of empty space away by opening not just one, but thousands of holes in it all at once. Just as firefighters did to a burning structure under pressure. They opened many outlets instead of just one.

The scientists a few years back had determined exactly what strange gravitational force was holding empty space together like a bubble, allowing a ship to enter and leave, yet holding the space together.

And once they had determined that force, they knew how to puncture the force to not so much let empty space out, but to let regular space and time flood in.

The entire bubble should, the scientists had told West, just vanish as if it had never existed.

West could only hope.

"Report status," West said to all the ships around the bubble ready to send a hundred probes each to open up holes.

A moment later Korgan looked up at him and nodded. "All eighty ships report green, Chairman."

West nodded, staring at the big screen in front of him showing nothing but empty space.

"Mission go," West said.

West knew that once he said that, a computer program from *Rescue One* would launch all probes at the exact same moment from all ships. West had been told that the probes would have a small charge when they hit the membrane, so it would look like eight thousand tiny lights flashing at the same time in a sphere shape in open space.

"Five seconds," Korgan said.

Intense, heavy silence filled the bridge of the ship.

West had no doubt not one word was being said anywhere in the large fleet of ships surrounding the empty space bubble.

West could not take his gaze for a second away from the massive screen in front of him.

Suddenly, there was a white flash of light from what looked like the surface of a sphere.

Then a moment later, the massive mother ship *Dreaming Large* appeared.

Cheering erupted around the bridge.

West just stood there grinning, staring at the screen, knowing that finally, after sixteen years, he would get to see his wife's face again. And maybe a little later actually hug her and kiss her.

After a moment, Korgan, a smile almost splitting his face, turned to West. "I have two chairmen of the *Dreaming Large* asking just what the hell is going on?"

West just smiled right back at Korgan. "Tell them to contact Chairman Ward and let him explain."

Then, for seemingly the first time in sixteen years, he went and sat down in his Chairman's chair.

And then on a private channel he said to *Rescue One*, "Please contact my wife on *Dreaming Large* and put her through to my personal screen here."

"I will be glad to, Chairman," *Rescue One* said.

"Thank you," he said.

And then, for the first time in sixteen years, he took a deep breath and relaxed.

~

USA Today **Bestselling Writer**

DEAN WESLEY SMITH

She Collected
Very Special Stones
For Very Special Memories

THE STONE SLEPT HERE

Jennifer Bends collects stones.

Special stones.

She puts her stones, both of them, on a shelf. No one asks her about the stones because the stones look plain, heavy, pointless.

But the stones contain memories.

Special memories.

And the stones contain a promise that only Jennifer and the stones know.

THE STONE SLEPT HERE

THE STONE DIDN'T look like much at first glance. Just a round rock, worn smooth through hundreds and hundreds of years of the blue waters of the Boise River moving over it.

Gray in color, even when wet and under bright sunlight, which was how Jennifer Bends found the stone when she was thirteen. She hadn't changed it at all. She liked it gray and round and simple.

She had been down on the riverbank under the Eagle Street Bridge with her mother and sister on a hot July day. The river water was cool, not cold, and not very deep. No real current existed where they waded since most of the river water went along the other tree-lined side.

The air of the late afternoon was hot, with little wind, but the river made everything smell fresh. And she was covered in suntan lotion, which she loved the smell of as well.

Where she found the rock was in a large pool of water that only came up to her knees. She had enjoyed just sitting in the pool, letting the cool water take away any thought of problems or boys in school or homework or how her mom barely afforded to buy them clothes and books.

When her hand touched the stone and she picked it up, she knew it was perfect. It was about the size of a sandwich. She fell in love with the stone at once. Smooth and warm and wonderful in her hand, she couldn't put it down.

And the stone was heavy enough to be important.

It always would remind her of that wonderful hot July afternoon on the river with her mother and older sister.

That day had been the best day they had had since her father had vanished earlier in the spring. Jennifer knew where he was, but she never told anyone, because her father had hurt her mother.

Now it was just Jennifer and her sister and her mom and that day along the riverbank proved they could be happy without their father.

Maybe a lot happier.

Jennifer took the stone home with her, even though her mother shook her head when she saw it.

Jennifer put it on her window ledge in her bedroom next to a similar large, gray stone. They could have almost been twins.

The two stones were always there, through junior high, then high school.

The two stones slept side-by-side when she came home from college and when she met Frank, the man she thought was the love of her life.

Jennifer had turned into an attractive woman, with short brown hair and large brown eyes. Men liked her, and she liked them, but staying with one just hadn't happened until Frank, the tall, strong, black-haired man with an easy smile and rough hands.

She got a job teaching grade school out of college and Frank worked at a tire store.

She moved the two stones to their new small starter home, just letting them rest on a shelf, occasionally holding up some books.

But then Frank turned out to be anything but a love of her life.

More like a monster of the night.

One month into their April marriage, she found out he was sleeping with another woman, an old girlfriend. And she asked him about it and he called her names she should not have been called.

No self-respecting woman should ever be called, actually.

And for a moment he looked like he might hit her as she stood her ground, facing him.

Then he had stormed out to go drinking and when he finally came home, almost too drunk to walk, she took the stone she had found in the river that wonderful day with her mom and sister and hit him over the back of the head with it when he wasn't looking.

He went down hard.

Out like a light.

No blood, thankfully.

She put a black plastic bag over his head, tied it off tight around his neck, then put another one over his head and tied it as well. Then she hit him in the head as hard as she could a few dozen more times with the stone.

The stone felt solid in her hands. After a time, Frank's head did not feel solid under the stone.

That was exactly as she had done with her daddy when he came home drunk that night after hitting her mother. She wanted to make sure he would never wake up.

Her daddy never woke up.

Frank would never wake up.

Then Jennifer washed her stone off carefully, with bleach, and put it back on the shelf next to the other stone.

Her father's stone.

With the help of a wheelbarrow that Frank had not understood why she wanted to buy, she got him out of the house and into his car, the black bag still securely wrapped around his head to make sure no blood got anywhere.

His car was a blue Mercedes that she had discovered after they were married that he couldn't afford on his salary at the tire store.

Driving very carefully, with him slouched in the passenger seat with a baseball cap over the bag on his head, she took him to the woods behind her mother's house and buried him next to her father.

It was the same spot she could see from her childhood window.

Her mother still lived there in that house.

The woods there were tall pine, with thick underbrush. A seldom-used dirt road went through the edge of the large stand of trees. The area had been declared wetlands and no one could build on it at all. Besides, Jennifer knew the neighbors around the wetlands liked the large area of trees and water and the small stream that flowed through the trees. It gave their neighborhood class.

Jennifer then put on a pair of Frank's coveralls he used at work. They were black with a few patches on them, so they would help her stay hidden in the dark. And she had brought old tennis shoes and an extra pair of socks to change into when finished.

It took Jennifer four hours of digging in the soft spring soil, but she got the job done and then covered up any sign that she had been there as best she could.

In a month or so, the underbrush would cover it all.

No one had found her daddy there. No one would find her husband either.

Then she took his car to a spot near their small starter home and parked it on the bank of the Boise River, pointing down into the fast river, roaring with the spring runoff. She smudged up the steering wheel and key to make sure both her prints and his prints were on the car.

She changed out of her dirt-covered shoes and walked on the rocks down to the river and tossed them in.

She took off his coveralls and tossed them on the front seat, opened both windows full, and made sure no one was around at all, anywhere.

Then she put the car in gear and let it go down the hill and into the fast water.

It tipped over at once and was swept away downriver, sinking out of sight in the dark water.

Staying in the shadows and hiding any time a car even came close, she walked the few blocks home. Then she made sure that there was no blood or anything showing on the hardwood floor where she had hit him.

No sign.

Nothing.

Then she kissed both rocks goodnight and went to bed.

The next day at school, she was called out of class with the bad news that they had found his car in the river. The two detectives asked her if he had come home last night.

She did her best to act like the worried wife, saying that he was angry when he left, despondent, went to drink. And had never come home.

The detectives told her that he had been drinking until about one in the morning and at which bar. She knew it was the one his old girlfriend worked at.

They told her there were tire tracks that matched his car going into the river near their home.

She told them that he loved that car, that they had only been married a month, and made them promise to do everything they could to find him.

Of course, a year later, no one had found him.

After two years, she filed for divorce and got it.

About that point, she started dating again.

It was during a wonderful trip with her new boyfriend to the Oregon Coast that she found the third rock.

Her boyfriend named Craig knew about how Frank had vanished, leaving her a month after they had married. He treated her with respect and a gentle touch.

And he didn't drink.

He was the one, actually, that found the stone for her.

He came up to where she sat on the beach in a lounge chair, staring at the beautiful ocean. He was holding a stone about the same size as the other two she had in her collection.

The new stone was smooth like her other two, worn down through time in the water. It also was plain and simple and felt important when she held it in her hand.

"It's perfect," she had said, smiling up at him. "Just perfect."

"I hoped you would like it," he said.

"I like it more than you can imagine," she said, kissing him.

And when they got back to Boise, she put the rock on her fireplace mantle with her other two rocks.

They all slept together there, looking peaceful.

Six months later, she and Craig were married.

So far things were going smoothly.

So far.

Some Classic Dean Wesley Smith Stories
Available at your favorite booksellers.

Now Available
from all your favorite booksellers
in trade paper and electronic editions.

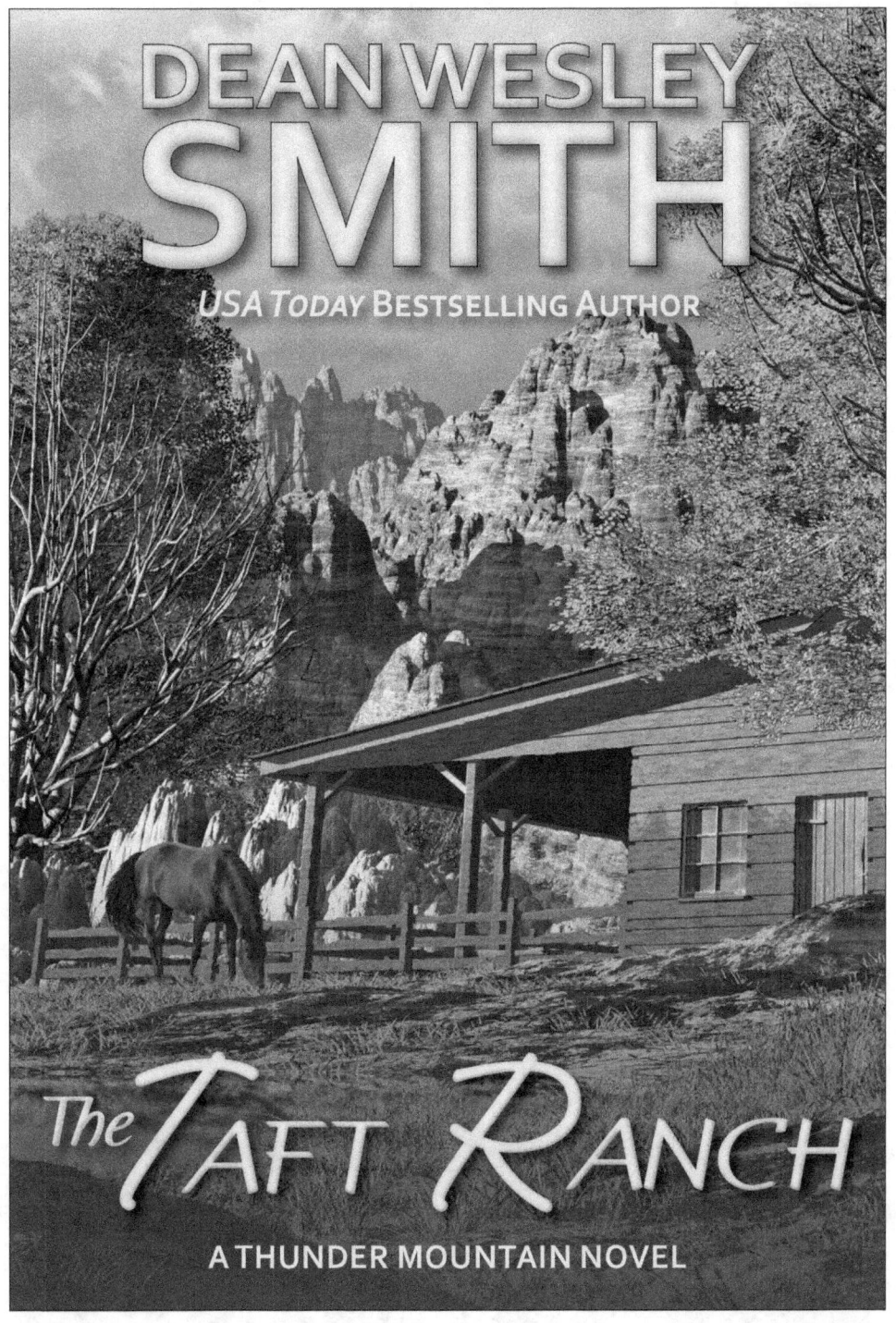

FREEZEOUT

A COLD POKER GANG MYSTERY

DEAN WESLEY SMITH

USA TODAY BESTSELLING AUTHOR

Sandy Hunter kissed her husband goodbye one normal morning on her way to work. She never made it. Last seen walking alone into a Las Vegas hotel room, she never came out and no sign of her remained in that room.

Her missing person's case went cold for fourteen years until retired Las Vegas detectives Debra Pickett and Sarge Carson, members of the Cold Poker Gang, decided to investigate how a woman could vanish from a locked hotel room without a trace.

Another twisted Cold Poker Gang mystery from the prolific mind of USA Today *bestselling writer Dean Wesley Smith. If you love puzzle mystery novels, grab a Cold Poker Gang mystery novel.*

FREEZEOUT
A Cold Poker Gang Novel

PART ONE
The Game Starts

PROLOGUE

March 3rd, 2002
Las Vegas, Nevada

SANDY HUNTER KISSED her husband Rich goodbye in the modern kitchen of their apartment four blocks from Las Vegas University campus. Everything seemed perfectly normal. The morning sun through the kitchen window promised a beautiful spring day and that evening they had date night planned, with a wonderful dinner at their favorite sushi place.

Sandy stood five-two on a good day and looked much taller because she always wore heels, slimming black slacks, and had her medium-length brown hair pulled up on the top of her head. At twenty-four, she was just finishing her second master's degree in business. She worked part time at a securities firm and to everyone around her she appeared to be happy.

She and Rich had many plans for the future.

Rich still had a year to go on his second master's in history and was working at the university. He hoped to eventually become a professor there after a number of years.

He was short at five-five and Sandy often looked taller, something he didn't mind in the slightest. Unlike her, he didn't much care about his height one way or another.

Sandy told Rich she would be home to change clothes before dinner, then went down the three flights of stairs and got into their new Toyota two-door.

Security cameras showed that she pulled out of the apartment complex parking lot, turning toward Las Vegas Boulevard. In normal traffic, it would take her fifteen minutes to get to her office off Charleston. The morning's traffic was normal, as far as the radio said.

She had a meeting in forty-five minutes and had told Rich she wanted to go early to prepare. She had told her co-worker the same thing and they planned on meeting over coffee and Danish rolls thirty minutes ahead of the meeting.

She never arrived at work.

Just before the meeting started her co-worker called Rich to see if Sandy was sick or had forgotten the meeting. Both Rich and the co-worker were instantly worried that Sandy had gotten into a wreck.

After three hours of waiting and calling hospitals and no word, Rich finally called the police. They could do nothing, but a friendly detective listened to Rich and believed him and then called Sandy's office to confirm. Clearly something had happened to Sandy, so the police put out a notice to watch for Sandy's car.

At seven in the evening, Sandy's car was found parked in the Bennington Hotel and Casino underground parking lot just off the Strip. The hotel security cam showed Sandy pulling into the lot seven minutes after she left home, locking her car, and walking calmly into the hotel.

She seemed to know where she was going and was in no hurry.

She went to an elevator, and got off on the eleventh floor. She used a key card she pulled from her small clutch purse to open the door to a room halfway down the hallway.

The room was reserved in the name of Rich Hunter, Sandy's husband, and paid for with his credit card.

Rich swore he knew nothing about it and a check of their financial records showed that was the only time such a charge had been made on either of their cards.

Sandy's behavior was very, very unusual, to say the least. Yet she seemed to be acting normally.

Almost as if she did this every day.

At two in the morning, when the police knocked on the hotel room door, no one answered and the room was empty.

The security cameras showed that no one had left that room after Sandy entered.

And no one had gone in ahead of her either.

The room had been reserved online.

Sandy had left no fingerprints in the room, but the prints from the previous couple who had stayed there were everywhere. Nothing had been wiped down or cleaned beyond the normal maid service.

There were no leads and her missing person's case went quickly cold, with only her husband trying to find out what happened to his wife.

No one had any idea why Sandy Hunter vanished.

Or how a person could simply vanish from a major Las Vegas hotel room without a trace.

ONE

November 16th, 2016
Las Vegas, Nevada

RETIRED LAS VEGAS Detective Debra Pickett stood sipping a cup of black coffee, without cream, in the kitchen of her penthouse condo in the Ogden in downtown Las Vegas.

Outside her windows, she could tell the late fall day was shaping up to be another beautiful day. The forecast said the high temperature today would be around seventy.

Perfect. She loved the Vegas spring and fall weather. Comfortable during the day, cool at night.

She stood five-feet-four and had brown hair that she kept short and styled because it was just a bunch easier to deal with every day.

She had on jeans, a cotton blouse, and a light sweater. She had her badge in a holder on her belt covered by her sweater and her service gun in a holster under her arm. She would hide that with a light-brown jacket when she went out.

She and Retired Detective Ben "Sarge" Carson were headed for their normal morning walk along Fremont Street to the Golden Nugget buffet for breakfast. He owned the penthouse condo beside hers. And she had spent the night there, as was becoming wonderfully normal.

Sometimes he stayed with her, but she liked his place even better than her wonderful condo, if that was possible, so the last few weeks they had spent every night in his condo.

She had a fresh cup of coffee sitting on the counter beside her, waiting for him to finish dressing and come over to get her. She had gotten out of the shower first and rousted his handsome body out of bed.

Sarge had thick gray hair and for sixty was in the best shape of any man she had ever seen or been with. Even when she was younger.

On the floor at her feet, a young black and white kitten she affectionately referred to as Nose worked on her morning treat. Nose stayed the night with her at Sarge's place, sometimes sleeping on the bed with them, sometimes running through the condo playing with his two kittens, Pete and Ree. Ree was short for Repeat.

Both his cats were orange tabbies and they looked a lot alike. He had started from the moment he picked them up at the pound calling them Pete and Repeat until he thought of better names. She couldn't save them from the original names no matter how many names she suggested, so at least they had shortened the little one's name to Ree.

And Nose hadn't been her cat's name to start with either. She had called her Cleo, but she had the cutest little white button nose and sometime during the first week after they got the cats, Nose stuck that white button nose into a place it shouldn't be during a human sexual moment.

It seemed the nose was cold and wet and made Sarge shout and then laugh and from that moment onward the cat was stuck with Nose as a name.

Last night, at the Cold Poker Gang poker game, she and Sarge and Pickett's partner Retired Detective Robin Sprague had gotten a new case to work on.

At this point, there were fourteen retired detectives in the Cold Poker Gang, but only about ten showed up for the game on any given Tuesday. She and Sarge and Robin had decided they wouldn't miss a night, they loved it that much.

Before the tunnel case last month, Pickett and Robin had been partners. All through their detective years and afterwards they had been partners and Pickett could never imagine that changing. But with the tunnel case and meeting Sarge, he had become the third member of their team

All three of them loved working the cold cases and working together. Before they retired, none of them seemed to have enough time for many cold cases. That's why the Las Vegas police chief had given the Cold Poker Gang special status to work on cold cases. They could all still carry their guns and their badges. They just didn't get paid.

Having an unpaid group of experienced detectives volunteering to work cold cases freed up the on-duty detectives to do the more pressing work and allowed Las Vegas to now have one of the top-rated levels of closing cold cases in the entire country.

Besides that, no member of the gang had to do any paperwork. And none of them wanted the credit, so they often gave the credit to the working detectives, which kept the working detectives on the side of the Cold Poker Gang as well.

Pickett considered all this the best of both worlds. She could work at her own pace, do the job she still loved, and not have to do paperwork.

She had retired and gone to police heaven, or as Sarge liked to say, "a police fantasy world."

She liked the fantasy, especially working with Robin and now the man she was falling completely in love with.

This week, Retired Detective Andor Williams, the Cold Poker Gang's official contact with the chief of police, had given the three of them a cold case disappearance from March 2002. Pickett remembered something about it being one of the stranger cases she had heard about, but it had been a University Station case and Sarge remembered more about it since that had been where he was based at the time.

Normally, after a Cold Poker Gang meeting, she and Robin and now Sarge went out for dinner to discuss the case, but Robin had a late dinner party she had to go to with her husband, Will, and had to leave the game early. So Sarge and Pickett had promised her they wouldn't even look at the case until they met her at breakfast this morning.

So it was going to be a fun morning. New cases always excited Pickett.

Nose was finished with her morning treat, so Pickett picked up the dish and washed it off, then picked up the kitten and scratched her ears until she purred.

A new case to solve, a new kitten to pet, and a wonderful man in her life. Just didn't get much better.

TWO

November 16th, 2016
Las Vegas, Nevada

RETIRED LAS VEGAS Detective Ben "Sarge" Carson finished dressing and made sure that both of his cats had eaten some of their morning treats. They had and were now safely in his living room stretched out on the floor in the sun.

He had really come to love those two and Pickett's cat as well. Wonderful personalities that filled what had been a large, empty condo. Of course, having Pickett in and out and staying over every

night made this place feel like a home, of that there was no doubt.

He had dressed in his normal jeans and dress shirt. He kept his badge where it always had been, on his belt on his right hip and his gun in a carry holster under his arm.

For a few years after retiring he hadn't had his badge or his gun, but now that he was back with the Cold Poker Gang, it felt like he was again fully dressed. His entire identity was being a detective and he loved the fact that he didn't have to change that identity now that he was retired.

He put on a light jacket to cover the gun and the badge and then told the two kittens to behave. As cats do, they didn't even notice he was leaving as he went out into the penthouse foyer and then into Pickett's condo. The building had three penthouse condos. His was the largest, with an upstairs area that gave him almost a three hundred degree view of the city and the surrounding hills around Las Vegas.

After he had discovered that Pickett lived next door to him, he had looked into who owned the third one. It was owned by an older couple in Boise who only came to Las Vegas twice a year. The best kind of neighbor.

Pickett had gotten the money for her condo when her husband had a midlife crisis and left for Los Angeles with his thirty-year-old secretary. Sarge had gotten the money for his condo as just a tiny part of his inheritance when his father died four years ago. For retired detectives, they both lived in style. But except for the condos, you could never tell they both had money.

Pickett was holding her cat Nose when he came in. She smiled at him and nodded to the cup of coffee waiting for him on the counter. This was part of their routine that had developed in just a few weeks of knowing each other. She made them coffee in her place and then they walked the four blocks up to the Golden Nugget buffet for breakfast.

He liked the routine a great deal.

He scratched Nose's ears, then leaned against the counter and sipped his coffee. On the counter behind him was the gray folder with the details about their new case.

"You didn't peek at it, did you?" he asked, smiling at Pickett.

"I wanted to, but nope," she said, putting Nose on the ground. Nose stretched and then headed for the tan cloth couch in the living room area to stretch out in the sun.

"I'm kind of excited about this one," he said.

And he was. He remembered it being a real puzzle from his days on the force when it came up. He hadn't caught the case, but the two detectives who had been assigned the case wanted to bang their heads against a wall at times.

"What do you remember about it?" she asked.

"Sort of a locked room mystery," he said. "I remember a woman who had no business in a major hotel going into the room and never coming out. No sign of her ever being in the room was ever found. Or something like that."

Pickett smiled and looked at the folder. "Robin would kill us if we opened it without her."

Sarge laughed. Robin Sprague had been Pickett's partner for years on the force. They were known as two of the best detectives ever. Robin was married to Will Sprague who owned and ran the city's biggest private protection firm. Robin was an expert on computers and she also had all of Will's people to back her up when needed. And on some cases they really needed the computer work. The three of them were

lucky to have that kind of power at their disposal, that was for sure.

When on the regular force, Pickett had liked to do the legwork while Robin did the computer work. Sarge joining them had just given Pickett some company and cover when out knocking on doors and interviewing people. That was how he had done things as well.

He downed the rest of his coffee and rinsed out his cup in the sink, then turned to Pickett. "Let's get to breakfast before one of us opens that file."

Pickett rinsed out her cup and picked up the file. "How come I feel like a kid at Christmas about ready to open a present?"

"Because we're both warped, that's why," Sarge said, kissing her lightly and then helping her on with her jacket.

Now, walking down the street, they would look like a younger retired couple out for a walk. And Sarge liked the fact that they were a couple a great deal.

THREE

November 16th, 2016
Las Vegas, Nevada

PICKETT ENJOYED THE morning walk in the cool air. It made her feel alive and being alive and happy at the age of sixty-one would not have been something she would have bet would happen ten years earlier.

And walking with Sarge just made it all the better. Their strides seemed to match and she found she laughed a lot while with him.

At the top of the escalator going into the Golden Nugget buffet, she could see Robin already seated and eating at their favorite morning table.

The buffet was separated from the escalator area by a wall of plants and fake windows. The dining area was huge with at least seventy or more tables in three sections. Everything was decorated in brown and brass tones. Not gaudy like some restaurants in Vegas. Pickett thought it was comfortable, actually.

And the smell of ham and omelets made her instantly hungry.

It was her turn to pay and she did, then headed for Robin who looked up and smiled.

Robin had been her best friend for longer than Pickett wanted to think about.

Robin was solid, with square shoulders that showed all the time that she spent in a pool exercising. She had short, silver-gray hair and always wore a baseball cap that was now sitting on a chair beside her. She had on her dark windbreaker that Pickett knew concealed her gun and badge.

Robin was the smartest woman Pickett knew. But what she loved about Robin was that she didn't show the fantastic intelligence unless needed and never flaunted the fact.

Pickett dropped the file on the table near Robin. "No, we did not look, but you can while we get something to eat."

"Oh, fun," Robin said, pulling the file toward her.

Sarge laughed. "As I said, we're all strange."

"And that's news how?" Robin asked, smiling at them.

Ten minutes later Pickett had her slice of ham, scrambled eggs, and orange juice and was back at the table sitting across from Robin. Sarge was waiting for an omelet to be made. He usually had an omelet and a small waffle and orange juice.

They both had another cup of black coffee waiting for them at the table that Robin had signaled the waitress to bring.

Robin looked like she was about halfway through the report and her food was going untouched.

"Better eat," Pickett said.

"Wait until you read this," Robin said, surfacing and taking another bite of her scrambled eggs. "It's going to be damned impossible unless we get a really lucky break."

"Oh, great, one of those," Pickett said.

Actually, that excited her. Challenges were frustrating, sure, but great fun now that their entire careers didn't depend on solving the case.

"This case was cold from moment one," Robin said, shaking her head.

"What's Will up to?" Pickett asked, changing the subject off the case until Sarge got there.

"He and his people have a big convention to help protect some special guests," Robin said, shrugging. "But it's going well so he's been home every evening this last week."

"Can your marriage stand that?" Pickett asked, laughing. She knew that Will and Robin's marriage was about as strong as it came.

"Thank god for this case," Robin said, patting the paper in front of her. "Just what the marriage counselor ordered."

At that moment Sarge joined them and Robin had to get an update on the kittens. A detailed update, which allowed all three of them to get through most of the first round of their breakfasts.

Then Robin handed the first five pages of the report to Pickett and went back to reading.

Pickett read the first page and slid it to Sarge.

As Robin said, this case had been cold from the start.

A stable, happy woman named Sandy Hunter one morning doesn't show up for work. She is seen on security cameras entering the Bennington Hotel from the parking garage. She is then seen using a key card to get into a hotel room. No way of knowing how she got the card since she did not go to the front desk to get it.

Yet she had it.

She vanished the moment she entered the room and the door closed.

No security coverage showed anyone going or coming from the room except maid service earlier in the morning three hours before she arrived.

After Sandy Hunter, the next time that door was opened was when a detective named Carl Bower from the University Station showed up at the door with a manager. They opened the door and there was no sign the woman had been in the room.

The room was checked for blood and fingerprints and everything came up negative. And no way she could have gone out a window. The room was on the seventh floor and there was no ledge outside the window and the window had a secure feature on it that wouldn't allow it to open very wide.

Security showed Sandy Hunter clearly going into that room.

Every minute of every security footage from every camera of the hotel was scanned looking for her after that. No security tapes were tampered with either. Police and security checked and double-checked that.

It was impossible, but Sandy Hunter never left the building.

She vanished from a locked room without a trace.

When Pickett finished reading the report, she looked up at Robin who was sitting staring off into space.

They were supposed to solve cold cases, but this one was so cold, it had ice caked on it.

Layers and layers of ice.

FOUR

November 16th, 2016
Las Vegas, Nevada

SARGE WAS THE last one to finish reading the report. When he did, he sat back, feeling sort of stunned. Around them the normal sounds of the buffet went on. People talking, a group laughing, and plates and silverware clattering. He loved this place. And he loved the food even more.

He remembered Detective Bower and his partner going round and round about this case. In the file it detailed out everything about Rich Hunter, the husband, Sandy's job, and Rich's family. They got Sandy's email files from both home and work.

They came up with a big fat nothing.

There was no reason that Sandy Hunter, on her way to work for an important meeting, would stop at a hotel, use a key card no one knows how she got, and go into a room simply to vanish into thin air. No signs she was having an affair, no signs that she was unhappy in her marriage or her job.

And no signs at all of her in the fourteen years since she vanished.

"So what the hell happened to her?" Sarge asked, looking up at Pickett and then at Robin.

"I bet dead," Robin said. "But damned if I know why or how."

"Maybe kidnapped for sex trade," Pickett said. "She was good-looking enough from the pictures in the file. But how, no idea."

Sarge nodded. "I can see why Bower banged his head against the wall on this one."

"You know Bower?" Pickett asked.

Sarge nodded. "Nice guy, lost his partner about a year after this and decided to stay at a desk until retirement. Gained a lot of weight I hear. Retiring next year."

Robin pulled out a notebook and so did Pickett. Sarge took his from his inside jacket pocket. He used a small flip-page notebook, Pickett used a similar style with a stiffer cover, and Robin had a full spiral-bound notebook.

"So you two get to talk with Bower, see if there's more that's not in the report," Robin said.

Sarge nodded, but he doubted there would be. Bower had been one of the most organized detectives Sarge had ever met, which is why Bower could leave the streets without a problem. He liked the paperwork and every report he ever did was complete.

But Bower might have an opinion and that would be worth the time to talk.

Pickett glanced at Sarge, then turned to Robin. "Why do I have a hunch this isn't an isolated incident?"

"Just one that was caught quickly," Sarge said nodding. "If the police hadn't been ahead of normal procedure on this, someone would have already checked into that room the next day."

"I'll see what I can come up with about people vanishing out of hotel rooms," Robin said, making notes. "But we all know the hotels are extremely private about this sort of thing. Hell, if someone dies in one of their top suites, they move the body so as to not lose the room rental."

Sarge nodded and managed not to smile at how angry Robin sounded about that. Clearly she and Pickett had run into that a few times over the years. Every Las Vegas detective had.

"So we find and talk with the husband and the coworkers," Pickett said, taking the names and old contact information from the file and writing it in her notebook.

"Robin," Sarge asked, "would it be possible to track missing person cases through the police files with references to last time seen in a hotel? Just general."

"There will be a lot of those," Robin said, nodding and writing. "But we can figure out ways to narrow it down later. See if we have a pattern."

Sarge nodded. This was going to be the best they could do. A lot of this was going to be going back over ground already covered by Bower. But just maybe, with a little time, they might find something different.

Maybe.

He didn't hold out much hope on this case. On the small bar in Lott and Julia's basement where the Cold Poker Gang met and played cards once a week, there were four files. All still unsolved.

Sarge bet this one would be the fifth.

FIVE

November 16th, 2016
Las Vegas, Nevada

PICKETT LIKED DETECTIVE Bower almost instantly. He had his own office that looked out over a parking lot, which in Vegas was a normal view. His office was fairly large and clean and organized. He had family pictures of his wife, kids, and grandkids hanging on the wall.

He was a heavyset man as Sarge had said, going toward round. But his smile reached his dark eyes and he had a laugh that made people around him want to laugh along. He had on a white dress shirt and no tie and had his suit jacket hanging on a tree-stand near the door.

Pickett would have never figured him for a detective. More like an accountant.

Sarge introduced her and Bower and Sarge exchanged a few old laughs, then Bower indicated they should take a seat in front of his metal desk and he went around behind it and settled into an oversized leather chair that clearly wasn't department issue, but fit his large frame.

"So you two working a cold case for the Cold Poker Gang, huh?" Bower asked, smiling.

"We are," Sarge said.

"If I wasn't going to be so happy to get out of this job next year, I might think about joining the gang. That would be if they needed someone to do some behind the scenes stuff. Not much good out on the streets these days."

He laughed and patted his rounded stomach barely held in by his white dress shirt.

"The gang can use all the help it can get," Sarge said. "In all ways."

Pickett just nodded.

Bower smiled at that and nodded. "So I assume it's one of my old cases you're working on."

"The Sandy Hunter disappearance."

Pickett was surprised at Bower's reaction. He actually laughed.

"You folks take the hard ones, huh?" Bower asked, shaking his head. "That might be the quickest cold case I ever got. She vanished, but she couldn't. She was there but she shouldn't have been. No family problems, no issues at work. Nice woman, actually happy in life from what we could tell."

"Yet she was there and she did somehow get out of that room," Pickett said. "Got any theories how?"

Bower laughed again. "That kept me awake at nights. I have no flipping idea what happened in there. If I believed in aliens, I would say they beamed her up."

"Room was that clean?" Sarge asked.

"Completely," Bower said. "She walked in that door and didn't touch a thing. Nothing. I'm not kidding. Aliens or Captain Kirk beamed her into orbit."

They sat there in silence for a moment, then Pickett grabbed her notebook. "I got an idea who we might talk with."

Both Sarge and Bower looked at her.

"We need to talk with a hotel architect," she said, "get the plans for that floor and have an expert go over them."

Bower nodded. "Good idea. We didn't do that."

Sarge was sitting staring just over Bower's head at the wall.

After a moment Bower smiled at Pickett. "Does he do this a lot?"

Before Pickett could answer, Sarge came back into his eyes, then said, "Bower, you said that Hunter was there, but she shouldn't have been. Could that have been someone else?"

"The woman getting out of Hunter's car in the hotel parking garage was wearing the same clothes Hunter had on when leaving home," Bower said. "Same hairstyle, same height, same weight. So it if wasn't her it would have to be a pretty amazingly close double."

"But it would be possible?" Pickett asked.

Bower again laughed. "I think aliens might be possible. Double or not, she didn't walk out of that room."

"And she didn't fly," Sarge said.

"She didn't walk, she didn't fly," Pickett said, "but maybe she crawled. Through a vent or something."

Pickett wished at that moment she had a picture of the look on the two men's faces as they sat there thinking.

Priceless.

SIX

November 16th, 2016
Las Vegas, Nevada

SARGE HAD ENJOYED seeing Bower and some of the others around his old headquarters. But he didn't miss being there at all. They all looked too busy and far too stressed. And he remembered that feeling well.

He didn't miss it.

He liked what he was doing now and he really loved being with Pickett. Her idea of someone crawling out a vent in that hotel was stunning. A long-shot, but stunning.

When they got back to her Grand Cherokee SUV, she didn't even have to start it to turn on the air-conditioning. The slight warmth inside felt good against the chill of the morning air.

She took out her phone and called Robin.

Sarge got out his notebook again so he could write down thoughts and notes they would need.

Pickett put her phone on speaker and Robin answered by asking, "You get anything from Bower?"

"Nothing solid," Pickett said. "But Sarge came up with an idea while talking with him. Can you get the security footage of Hunter leaving her apartment and compare it with the security footage of her going into the hotel?"

Silence for a second on the other end, then Robin said, "Think it might be an imposter?"

"We have the equipment now to find that out," Pickett said, "unlike what they had fourteen years ago."

Sarge nodded to that. It was stunning the advancement in computers in the last fourteen years when it came to facial recognition and everything. And casinos had some of the best technology in the world in those areas to stop known cheaters and criminals.

And it was the casinos that had paid for and updated the police along the way with the same technology. One of the many things not publicized about the casinos helping the city and police.

"I'll get one of Will's experts right on that," Robin said. "Walk patterns, everything, we should know for sure in a couple of hours."

"Great," Pickett said. "Can you access the plans to the hotel area she disappeared in? We're going to go talk with James."

Sarge had no idea who James was, but clearly James and Pickett and Robin were on a first-name basis.

"Think she crawled out, huh?" Robin asked. "I'll dig up the plans."

"I'll call James and see if he is available to meet us, then let you know to send the plans to him."

"Will do," Robin said. "Good ideas."

And she hung up.

Pickett clicked off the phone, then dialed another number.

"James," she said. "It's Debra."

"Wonderful," Pickett said after a moment. "Loving the condo. Got an official job-favor to ask of you."

She waited for a second, then smiled at Sarge and said, "Yeah, Cold Poker Gang business."

Sarge was enjoying watching Pickett. One of the many things he really was coming to love about her was how animated she was when she talked. She talked with her hands and head and body movements, even when on the phone. He had no doubt he could just sit and watch her for hours on end.

"Would you take a look at some hotel plans for us?" Pickett asked. "We got a person who vanished out of a hotel room without a trace."

Pickett sat quiet for a moment, her eyes getting bigger and bigger.

"Didn't know that," she said.

Sarge wanted to ask What? What? What? like a little kid, but said nothing.

She nodded a few times. "Thanks, we appreciate it. I'll have Robin send the plans. We'll see you in about twenty minutes."

She clicked off her phone, dialed Robin, said, "Send them." And then hung up again, putting the phone in her pocket.

"Didn't know what?" Sarge asked.

"James said that kids are lost out of locked hotel rooms all the time," she said. "Often never found, sometimes found dead in ducts and plumbing areas and elevator shafts in large hotels. They go in, get lost, and can't get out and no one thinks to look for them inside the walls and ceilings."

Sarge just shook his head. Over the years he had heard about a few cases like that, but always thought it something unusual, not common.

"James said it's almost impossible, however, for a full-sized adult to get into those areas. Accesses are too small for the most part."

Sarge glanced down at his notes. "Sandy Hunter was only just over five feet tall."

Pickett started the car and headed out of the parking lot. For the next minute they both rode in silence.

They might have figured out how Hunter got out of the hotel room. But that was a long, long way from answering why?

And what happened to her?

SEVEN

November 16th, 2016
Las Vegas, Nevada

PICKETT REALLY LIKED James Newell and his wife Patty. Two of the nicer people who had ever lived as far as Pickett was concerned.

James had been the major partner of an international architecture firm based in Las Vegas. He had retired ten years before, but had helped Pickett and Robin on numbers of cases over the years. Pickett and Robin had had many wonderful dinners with him and Patty, as well as the fact that he had helped them solve three cases along the way.

His home was on a seven-acre estate sitting on a rock knoll outside of Vegas, completely protected by a tall decorative fence. The house looked like it fit near the peak of the hill, tucked in and among the huge desert rocks like it had grown there, not been built.

The natural wood and brown tones also helped it fit in. Huge windows looked back out over the valley and the city.

"Wow, this is something," Sarge said as Pickett got them through the gate and headed up the narrow, winding brown-paved road toward the house. The road wound around large rocks and brush like a stream flowing down a narrow canyon.

On the way to the house, she had told Sarge about James and Patty, about how they were good friends, and about how his firm had designed some of the major hotels and buildings around the world.

James greeted them at the large wooden front door with a smile. It had been months since Pickett had seen him and she gave him a big hug before introducing him to Sarge.

James stood tall and distinguished, with a full head of gray hair, long by anyone's standards. His face was full of wrinkles, but mostly from smiling Pickett was sure. The man loved to smile and laugh at most anything.

He had on his normal tan cloth slacks, a tan golf shirt, and tan socks without his normal loafers. Pickett couldn't remember ever seeing him in anything else. Even at major charity events. Patty would dress up, but he would wear the same thing, only adding a tan sweater at times.

When you were that rich and that successful, Pickett figured he could do anything he wanted. He once told her that everyone thought architects were strange, so he just played the part.

"Patty sends her regrets that she missed you," James said as he led them through the fantastic home to an office in the back. The home was made of all natural stone and wood and even though slightly bare, felt welcoming.

Sarge was just sort of staring at things as they walked, his mouth open slightly.

"I just looked at what Robin sent a moment before you got here," James said, indicating that they should watch a white wall. "So we can go over it together."

He clicked a couple keys on a computer terminal and the plans of the hotel came up on a large, blank wall. It was clearly projected on the wall by a projector hidden above it in the ceiling.

It made every room on the hotel plan large and the hallways look huge. Fantastic detail for looking at a plan.

"This is the floor Robin said the woman vanished from in 2002," James said. "Let me highlight the room in green that Robin said she went into."

A moment later one room turned green.

At that moment Pickett's cell rang. It was Robin.

Pickett clicked it on and then put it on speaker and held out the phone. "We're here with James."

Now Available
from all your favorite booksellers
in trade paper and electronic editions.

"Thanks, James, for helping us on this," Robin said.

"Just getting started," James said. "And Patty sends her best wishes."

"Back at her," Robin said. "And as far as the woman who went into that room you guys are going to study, it was Sandy Hunter. No questions."

Pickett glanced at Sarge who was looking shocked. On the way out to James' house, they had both figured Hunter had been kidnapped before getting to the hotel and switched out.

"One-hundred percent?" Pickett asked.

"One-hundred percent," Robin said. "Bye, James. You guys have fun."

And with that Robin hung up.

"Not what you expected, huh?" James asked.

Pickett just shook her head. "Not at all."

She looked back at the giant floor plan projected on the wall and the green room highlighted on the plan.

What in the world had happened in that room?

And more importantly, why?

EIGHT

November 16th, 2016
Las Vegas, Nevada

SARGE WAS STUNNED at the natural beauty of James' home.

The lobby had stone and rough wood and yet it felt warm somehow. And the office he had led them to was huge, the size of two large master bedrooms. Built-in bookshelves covered one wall, another wall was nothing but windows looking out over the valley. A large oak desk occupied one side of the room and some drafting boards and large computers filled another part.

James seemed like a great man, of that there was no doubt. And very willing to help. And Pickett sure seemed fond of him.

"Can we see the heating and cooling plans?" Sarge asked.

James smiled. "I'll lay them over the floor plan."

On the large image on the wall a maze of heating and cooling plans ghosted over the solid floor plan.

"Is that all through the ceiling?" Pickett asked.

"It is," James said, "and no access into it through anything larger than a small vent in the room."

"So heating and cooling is out," Sarge said, feeling disappointed.

"Not really," James said. "This shows all the ducts for delivering the air. Let me clear that off and show you the return-air system. Keeping air moving in a large building is a critical factor. And damned hard to calculate. The newer hotels keep each room or suite as a unit because it's easier to regulate, but the hotels from this time period used central heating and cooling per floor."

The ghost image vanished and then larger ducts appeared, clearly in the walls. It was at that moment that Sarge noticed how thick a few of the walls were.

"Here is what a standard return air vent looks like in that room at that time," James said.

He showed on an area beside the plan a picture of a grated rectangle, clearly just inches from the floor.

"How many of them would be in the room she vanished from?" Pickett asked a moment before Sarge could.

"Two," James said. "Both near the floor. These are the grates children get into and get lost. Hotels do their best to keep them secured tight. Modern return air ducts have moved up near the ceilings, usually over the entrance area and don't ever go outside the room."

Sarge went over to get a better look at the system. The return air duct seemed to dump into a giant square area along with about a quarter of the rooms on the floor. "Does that have duct work in these areas?" Sarge pointed to the giant square.

"No," James said. "Open air flow. In this hotel there are four of those square room return flow catches. The heating and cooling unit for the floor is there beside it.

"Door into this room I assume," Pickett said.

"There is," James said. "All four of these have a door into the floor's service area."

"Besides getting out onto the same floor," Pickett asked, "are there other ways out of that service room?"

James laughed. "A number. Let me show you."

On the screen the return air ghost image vanished and the floor plan of the large service area in the center of the building came up.

Sarge could see that off that service room were the bank of elevators and also a large square area labeled plumbing."

"So you can get into the elevator service area," Pickett said, "and the plumbing service stack from the large service room on every floor?"

"Yes," James said. "Standard large building design. Especially for the time."

"So exits from every floor from the elevator service area and the plumbing service area?" Sarge asked.

"Yes," James said. "Plus through the roof service area and also all the way to the basement utility room, which is one floor below the parking garage."

"And I assume no security cameras in any of it," Pickett said, shaking her head.

"Likely only at the entrances of each service area, and I wouldn't even count on that in the basement."

Sarge looked around at James. "So a small woman, just over five feet tall, could have undone one of the return air grates and gone inside and put the grate back in place."

"Very easily," James said, nodding. "And with the type of locking screws, she could have screwed the grate back into place from the inside. The grates were designed for workers to move through the passages when needed for cleaning and pest control."

Pickett just laughed.

Sarge shook his head.

"She could have gone in there," Sarge said, "worked her way to the service room, into the elevator shaft and climbed down to the basement and left from there? Possible?"

"Very possible," James said.

Sarge nodded. Now they knew how Sandy Hunter got out of that room, but not any of the whys involved.

Pickett stared at the floor plan, then turned to James. "I know Robin got this plan easily and I'm sure you could have as well, but fourteen years ago, when this hotel was fairly new, who could have gotten the plans?"

James shrugged. "Plans are filed in public. Security areas and cage areas and finance areas are kept a tight secret for each casino, but hotel plans are public."

"So anyone," Pickett said.

"But the key is who would know that this was even possible?" Sarge asked.

James again just shrugged. "Any of the contractors. And on a project this size,

there would have been dozens of contractors not counting their employees. And you have to add in any architect or architectural student."

"So Sandy Hunter could have gotten this idea from a thousand different people?" Pickett asked.

James nodded. "At least."

Sarge just sighed and looked back at the floor plan projected on the wall. They had solved the mystery of how Sandy Hunter vanished from the room.

But now they were miles from finding out why she did this and what happened to her.

PART TWO
The Bets Go Up

NINE

November 16th, 2016
Las Vegas, Nevada

PICKETT CALLED ROBIN and told her to meet them at the Bellagio Café in twenty minutes for lunch.

"Got some fun stuff for you," Robin said.

Pickett laughed. "We got some stuff to share as well."

Then she got them down the narrow driveway that wound through the rocks and out onto the main road heading back into town. Sarge wasn't saying anything, just sort of staring off into space.

"A real puzzle isn't it?" Pickett asked.

"None of it makes any sense," Sarge said. "And that bothers me a lot. People do things for a reason. Money, love, hate, revenge, and so on. From what the file said about Sandy Hunter, there was no reason for her to do this."

Pickett agreed. Sarge hit on exactly what had been bothering her from the moment Robin said it was actually Sandy Hunter who went into that hotel room.

"So we dig until we find the reason," Pickett said.

Sarge nodded. "I think we take a run at the husband. He might think of something he hadn't thought important when he learns she did it on purpose. And clearly planned it."

"I agree," Pickett said. She wasn't looking forward to that conversation, but she knew Sarge was right, that was the next logical step.

The Bellagio Café had an atmosphere that Pickett flat loved. Brown tones of oak and cloth, with lots of plants between the booths to give each booth a sense of privacy.

The sounds of the casino were like a distant background and even the sound of others talking in the restaurant never seemed to get very loud.

She and Robin had often come here for lunch or dinner when out this far along the Strip. This was her second favorite place and had been happy to learn that it was Sarge's second favorite restaurant as well.

One of the big reasons was that not only was it comfortable, but the food was wonderful and the selection amazing at any time of the day or night.

She had learned from Sarge that Julia and Lott and Andor, the three retired detectives that ran the Cold Poker Gang, also came out here a great deal when on cases. They were nowhere to be seen at the moment.

She and Sarge got seated in a back booth with cloth seats, one of their favorite booths since the first case they met on. It was less than a month ago that she had spent a lot of time in this booth getting to know the handsome man sitting beside her. Now she couldn't imagine not having him beside her.

Amazing how her life had changed in just a short month.

Robin wasn't there yet, so both got coffee and water and menus.

They had both just started to look at the menu when Robin slid into her spot in the booth and put her notebook on the chair.

She had on a light pull-over jacket since the fall air still had a bite to it this morning. It looked police issue, but Pickett knew it wasn't.

"So who gets to go first?" Robin asked, smiling at the two of them.

Sarge laughed. "She seems excited, don't you think?"

Pickett also laughed. "She does. So please go ahead."

Robin smiled and opened her notebook.

"Your idea to check for patterns hit a gold mine," Robin said. "From 1998 until 2015, over ten thousand women have been reported missing and last seen in a hotel in Las Vegas."

"What?" Pickett asked, not even grasping that number.

Robin held up her hand. "Half of those were solved quickly, another quarter of them were run-away women, also solved. No one really missing with any of those. Many others were solved as well one way or another."

"So how many are still cold cases?" Pickett asked.

"About eight hundred," Robin said "over the seventeen years in all the hotels in Vegas. So I sorted for a woman's description matching Sandy Hunter. Size, shape, married, that sort of thing in those eight hundred. And I also took out any disappearance from a newer hotel."

Robin smiled at both of them. Pickett knew that smile. It was clear she had a lot of information and was loving every minute of this.

"So how many?" Sarge asked, shaking his head.

"Eighty-five cases," Robin said. "All similar. A woman who didn't ever go to a hotel or casino suddenly vanishes into one and is never seen again."

"Eighty-five?" Pickett asked. "That's stunning."

"It gets better," Robin said. "This is a picture of the eighty-five women."

She took out a sheet of paper with eighty-five small thumbnail-sized pictures of women on it. She slid it first to Pickett.

Pickett looked at it. The images were small, all the women looking right into the camera. Clearly driver's license pictures.

All the women had different haircuts and wore different clothing, but something about it seemed odd. She slid the paper to Sarge, who frowned looking at it.

Pickett could feel that something was wrong with the pictures, she just couldn't put her finger on what.

"Here is what I found when I ran the woman's pictures through a facial recognition software," Robin said.

She took out another page and slid it to Pickett.

It had five women on it, all about the same age.

Pickett looked at the smiling face of Robin and then slid the paper to Sarge who sort of snorted.

"All eighty-five missing women are actually only five women?" Pickett asked.

Robin nodded. "All between five foot tall and five-two."

"Any connections at all between them?" Sarge asked.

"All I have is their many married names," Robin said. "Seventeen married or fake names each, actually."

She pointed to the picture of Sandy Hunter. "I'm calling her March because

every March she goes missing. Ten times she was married, seven times only engaged. The others each have their own month to vanish."

Pickett sort of sat there stunned. She couldn't even begin to wrap her brain around this.

"Every March?" Sarge asked, his voice soft.

"Every March," Robin said. "She always had different hair color and background and all that. Different job, everything. But no doubt at all it was the same woman every March. The Sandy Hunter case was the only one that actually got her entering a room though. And that was only because Bower took pity on the husband and was ahead of procedure."

Pickett just sat there, stunned.

At that moment the waitress came to take their order, which was a welcome relief to Pickett as she tried to wrap her mind around why a woman would vanish seventeen times in seventeen years.

Five women, actually.

This case just kept getting stranger and stranger.

And bigger and bigger.

TEN

November 16th, 2016
Las Vegas, Nevada

SARGE GAVE HIS order to the waitress, but felt like he was almost sleepwalking. Why would the same five women set up a life and then disappear every year? In all his years of being a detective, he had never felt this stunned.

Robin was smiling and Pickett looked as shocked as he felt.

"It took me a good half hour to get past the idea that something like this could happen," Robin said. "And it's something that never would have been caught if we hadn't been trying to dig up leads on this one cold case."

Sarge nodded to that. No chance that any normal investigation would have run a search like Robin did, looking for patterns. Just never would have happened.

"So what's your news?" Robin asked.

Sarge nodded to Pickett that she should go ahead. He wasn't certain he could even focus on what they had discovered at the moment.

"James showed us how the woman got out of the hotel room," Pickett said. "Because she was so tiny and short, she fit into a return air duct. She went out through the ductwork into a maintenance room, then climbed down an elevator shaft to the sub-basement and went out through the parking garage, more than likely."

"All the security footage from the hotel for three days before and three days after still exist," Robin said. "I'll find out when she got out and now that I know they changed identity, I'll know what to search for."

Sarge nodded, then said what he was sure all of them were thinking. "Why?"

Robin nodded, as did Pickett.

"I have two of Will's best people searching through records of all the left spouses," Robin said. "They had gone through ten of them before I left and not a one reported anything at all missing when their wife vanished. Nothing out of checking, no credit card uses, nothing other than the jewelry and clothes they had on when they vanished."

Again Sarge just shook his head. Not a bit of this was making any sense at all.

"So we have five women," Pickett said, "getting into relationships that last exactly one year before they vanish and change identity."

"They all work regular jobs?" Sarge asked.

"From what we have found so far, yes," Robin said. "Sandy Hunter, our March woman, was pretty typical. Her next time out she worked housekeeping at a second hotel. The year after that she worked at a catering service. I will be working on tracing back their first run at this."

"See if you can find the connection between the five women," Sarge said.

"There has to be one," Pickett said.

At that point the food came and Sarge slowly came to grips with the crazy idea of all this as he ate a French dip sandwich with fries. By the time the waitress took his plate and refilled his coffee, he felt like his mind had returned a little.

"So here is what we know so far on this mess," Sarge said, opening his flip notebook. "First off, we know that the same five women, starting in 1998, vanish from a hotel and each do so on the same month every year."

Robin and Pickett both nodded.

"We are pretty certain that Hunter went out through a return air vent in a hotel room," Sarge said.

Again both women nodded.

Sarge looked at his notes and realized he didn't know one important fact. "Do they always vanish in the same hotel?"

"Three different hotels," Robin said. "They alternate around and all three hotels were built in the same period, so they all would have the same return air systems. But we can check that. I'll have a lot more by dinner. I even have Will

fascinated on this case, so he's throwing help at it. Right now he's got two computer specialists digging and has told me he's willing to get more at it if needed."

Sarge nodded. That was great to hear. Not much hid for long from Will and his security people and computer specialists.

Then it dawned on him what he had just thought. "Robin, these women are going to need to create new histories, new ids every year good enough to stand up to some heavy checking for jobs and a driver's license. How would they do that?"

"Shit," Robin said, flipping open her notebook and writing quickly. "There can't be a lot of people in this city who can do that level of work since 1998. I'll find out."

"So we are still about a thousand miles from the why of all this," Pickett said.

"A sick game to keep five women from becoming bored in life?" Robin asked.

Sarge shrugged. It might be just that, but he had a hunch there was something more going on.

Something much worse.

But he had no idea why he thought that.

ELEVEN

November 16th, 2016
Las Vegas, Nevada

PICKETT FELT BETTER, more grounded after a BLT sandwich. Over their coffee, they tried to figure out a way to find the motive on all of this. And what the women were even doing.

Robin would go back to her office and try to find out how long it took Sandy Hunter to leave the building after she vanished. And keep chasing any way of finding out how the five women might be connected.

Pickett and Sarge would head to the hotel and see if they could get a tour of the maintenance rooms on the floor Sandy Hunter vanished from. Sarge figured that if they saw the area, it might give them some ideas and Pickett agreed.

Then they all agreed Pickett and Sarge needed to contact and talk to the husband of Sandy Hunter, see if he has anything odd that he remembered. Pickett doubted they would get anything of value, but sometimes it was the smallest detail that broke open a case.

It only took them ten minutes from the Bellagio parking lot to the Bennington parking garage. They went up to the front desk and asked for a manager from security. Sarge flashed his badge and three minutes later a man by the name of Stevenson appeared. He looked to be in his early forties and clearly was management. His hair was balding and he wore a dark suit with a red tie. Pickett could tell he didn't miss a detail, the type of person who worked security in the big hotels.

In fact, she bet Stevenson could read a person across a room and would be dangerous in a poker game.

After introductions, Sarge detailed out what they were doing and wondering if they could see the maintenance area on the 11th floor.

"Can't see why not," Stevenson said. "Always glad to help the police, but if you wanted to see our security areas, I would have needed to get higher permission."

"We can understand that," Pickett said.

Stevenson asked a few quick questions on the elevator ride about the case they were working on. Both Pickett and Sarge said nothing about any other

women or regular disappearances. They just gave him the basics of the Sandy Hunter case.

When Stevenson heard the name Sandy Hunter, he laughed. "We get a lot of people who supposedly go missing in the casino, but on that one we still have an open file. You thinking maybe she went out through the return air system?"

"A theory," Pickett said. "That's why we would like to see the maintenance room."

"Only theory I ever had on it as well," Stevenson said, nodding. "But it was before my time here. If you end up solving it, would you let me know so I can close that file?"

"Glad to," Sarge said.

Stevenson waved to the security camera near the maintenance room door, then used a key card to unlock a blank door. It swung open and the lights came up.

The room wasn't that big, about the size of a small bedroom, and was mostly empty. Seven metal doors led off from the room, all closed.

Giant ducts covered the ceiling, all going to the left of the room and vanishing.

Each door was labeled and had no lock on them.

"Heating and cooling there," Stevenson said, pointing to the room where all the large ceiling ducts led. "Elevator there, plumbing stacks there."

He pointed at two doors across from them.

"Mind if we take a look at the elevator shafts?" Sarge asked.

Stevenson nodded and went and opened the door.

Pickett could see the ten elevator shafts. There was a metal ladder on both sides of the huge open area and as they watched from the doorway an elevator flashed upwards.

Below they could see the tops of a few elevators and below them the basement.

"We're thinking she climbed down to the basement and got out that way," Sarge said.

Stevenson nodded. "Doors locked from the outside down there but easy to go out."

"Any security in any of this?" Pickett asked.

"Only on the doors coming into here," Stevenson said.

Stevenson closed the door as another elevator flashed past. Pickett would have been scared to death climbing down that metal ladder, but she had little doubt she could do it if she needed to.

Stevenson went over to the other side of the room and opened a door. On the other side was a very stark room again the size of a small bedroom. From two sides massive ductwork entered the room just below the ceiling and a massive duct left the room going across the top of the maintenance room.

"They call this a return air cache," Stevenson said. "The air from a quarter of the rooms on this floor flow in here and then goes back to the heating system that pumps air back into the rooms. Even when no heat or air-conditioning is on, the air keeps flowing."

"I thought the return air grates in each room were at floor level," Pickett said, looking up at the massive ducts above them. Ladders built into the walls led up to each one.

"They are," Stevenson said.

"Ladders inside the ducts for maintenance?" Sarge asked.

Carson nodded.

"How often are these ducts cleaned?" Pickett asked.

"April and October," Stevenson said.

"You find things in the ducts?" Sarge asked.

"Oh, sure," Stevenson said, laughing. "Usually money, sometimes dirty movies or sex toys people have stashed behind the grates. One time, a couple years ago,

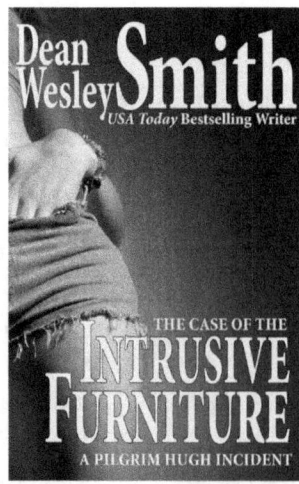

they found a wedding dress. Not at all sure what that was about. By the time the crew gets done with the entire hotel they have a lot I can tell you."

Pickett looked up at the ductwork. "Mind if I climb up and take a look?"

"No trouble," Stevenson said, pulling a tiny flashlight out of his pocket. "You'll need this to see much."

Pickett could tell that Sarge wasn't really pleased with that, but instead of saying anything, he moved to spot her as she climbed quickly up the ladder.

At the top she could sit up easily without bending over, the duct was that large. And she could feel a pretty good breeze blowing on her from the rooms.

She shined her light down the large duct and she could see where there was a hole going down and part of the large main duct turned in both directions.

"It's not all this big beside every room is it?" Pickett asked, looking down at Stevenson and the worried expression on Sarge's face.

"Oh, no," Stevenson said. "On the other side of that it branches and dozens and dozens of narrow ducts drop down to floor level along the hallway. It's an amazing maze."

"Too small for me to get through?" Pickett asked.

"Afraid so, Detective," Stevenson said. "The maintenance people who do those ducts can't be more than five feet tall. They are all women, actually."

"Your staff doesn't do the cleaning?" Sarge asked.

"Nope. But I can give you the company's name that does. They service a number of hotels around town."

Sarge glanced up at Pickett who just smiled. Then she said, "Coming down."

She turned back around and found the ladder rung and went carefully down with Sarge on one side and Stevenson on the other.

About as safe as a person could get on a ladder.

TWELVE

November 16th, 2016
Las Vegas, Nevada

SARGE AND PICKETT thanked Stevenson for the tour and the name of the cleaning service and headed down to the parking garage for her car. Once in the car, Sarge glanced at Pickett. He held up the name of the service. "You think these folks might have something to do with all this?"

Pickett laughed and took out her phone. "I sure think we should get Robin and Will's people looking into the business, don't you?"

She glanced at it, then said, "No reception."

She handed it to Sarge and got the SUV headed up and out of the parking garage. Once out of the garage, Robin drove for about a block before finding a spot to pull over near a construction site.

She called Robin and told her what they had found. Sarge listened but didn't add anything in. None of this was making sense to him still. Not a bit of it. They were looking at a few puzzle pieces and trying to get a large picture. Wasn't happening.

After Pickett got off the phone with Robin, she got them moving again toward an office at the University of Nevada Las

Vegas. Sandy Hunter's husband, Rich, taught there and was more than willing to talk with them about his missing wife.

About eight years ago he had had her declared dead and had gotten remarried. He now had two kids and from what Robin could find, seemed to be doing fine.

Sarge had suggested they not tell him anything about what they had found so far, just explain they were working on the case again because of the Cold Poker Gang.

The university area was full of large trees and shaded. Many of the trees hadn't lost their fall leaves yet so it still seemed lush, something Sarge enjoyed in the spring, summer, and fall. But today the shade made everything feel colder.

Professor Hunter's office was in an older brick building that had the feeling of an old library. His office was on the second floor and the wooden staircase in the building was wide and the wood smoothed almost white in the center of the stairs by so much traffic.

They knocked on the old wooden office door and a bald man with a wide smile greeted them, inviting them in and offering them chairs in front of his desk. Sarge wondered how many students over the last decade had sat in exactly those chairs.

Hunter was clearly a smart man who seemed, at least outwardly, happy. Kind of sad that a nice guy like him had been taken by whatever scam the five women were pulling.

"So you are looking into Sandy's disappearance after all these years," Hunter said as he sat down. "Can I ask why, detectives?"

Pickett explained how they were basically retired and on a special task force trying to solve old cold cases. Sandy's case had just come up.

"Not at all sure what I can add," Hunter said, "that I didn't already tell Detective Bower and his partner."

"We just want to look at everything again," Sarge said. "Sometimes time can bring up all sorts of things that seemed normal but through the perspective of time now seem odd. Anything like that?"

Hunter seemed to think for a moment, slowly shaking his head.

"When did you first meet Sandy?" Pickett asked.

Hunter shrugged. "About two years before she disappeared."

Sarge sat back, stunned at that.

Picket glanced at Sarge, then followed up her question before Hunter could tell anything seemed odd. "Were you dating that first year?"

"Oh, heavens, no," Hunter said. "I would just run into her on campus, usually about once or twice a month and we would talk. She didn't give me her address and phone number until about a year before she vanished and we were married eight months later."

Sarge slowly let out the breath he had been holding. These women found and set up their next relationships before vanishing from the previous one. Amazing.

Simply amazing.

And very damned cold-blooded.

"So did you ever meet any of Sandy's family?"

"All dead," Hunter said. "Back when she was a kid. She was raised in the system back east in Boston."

"She have friends?" Pickett asked.

"A few close friends from college and a few at work," Hunter said. "Everyone liked her. I loved her."

Sarge leaned forward slightly. "You ever meet the friends from college?"

Hunter shook his head. "They were scattered around the country, so never did even though she said she wanted me to meet them. I e-mailed them to let them know she was missing. Got a few e-mails back, but I kind of had the feeling they blamed me."

Pickett glanced at Sarge. He had a hunch they were both thinking the same thing, that her friends from college were the other four women.

"And you had no indication anything was wrong the day she vanished, or the weeks leading up to it?" Sarge asked.

"Nothing at all," Hunter said. "Everything was exactly as it had been those three months of marriage. She seemed happy, actually."

"And nothing vanished with her?" Pickett asked.

Hunter shook his head. "Just her clothes and her engagement and wedding ring is all, and whatever else she had in her purse. She seldom carried much money, liked to use her debit card for things."

"We talked with Detective Bower," Sarge said, "who said that her cards were never used. That right?"

Hunter nodded. "She vanished without a trace."

"You ever think you see her again around town?" Pickett asked.

Hunter laughed. "Oh, sure, for the first year or so I thought I saw her everywhere. But I was wrong every time. A counselor told me that was normal for people in my position."

Sarge didn't want to tell him that he might have been right a few of those times.

"So was she ever gone in the year you knew her?" Pickett asked.

Hunter sat back for a moment, clearly thinking back over time. "Yeah, she went to visit two of her college friends for five days a month after we met. Then in the fall she took another trip up to Seattle, I

think she said to stay with another friend there for five days, a month before our wedding. Said she was trying to convince her friend to come down and stand up for her in the wedding."

"She didn't, I assume," Pickett asked.

"Gloria, a friend from work, did the honors," Pickett said. "Might want to talk with Gloria if you can find her. She and Sandy seemed to have gotten very close. She might know more than I do."

They thanked Professor Hunter after a couple more questions and headed back out to Pickett's car without talking.

When Pickett closed her door, Sarge turned to her and asked, "Where do you think Sandy went on those two vacations?"

Pickett shrugged. "Not a clue. But I wouldn't bet against the timing being the same timing as that cleaning company cleaning out the vents in those two hotels."

Sarge just looked at her, surprised. "Why?"

Pickett shrugged as she got the car started. "No idea why. Not a damn bit of this is making any sense."

"Now that I agree with," Sarge said.

THIRTEEN

November 16th, 2016
Las Vegas, Nevada

PICKETT CALLED ROBIN from the car and she didn't have much yet, but would meet them for dinner at the buffet at Golden Nugget. The only time the three of them went there was while they were on a case. It felt almost like an office to them.

Sarge and Pickett spent the next hour talking with Gloria, Sandy's friend. Gloria had not aged well which had to do with the almost two hundred pounds she had gained since she knew Sandy.

And Gloria knew even less than Rich had known about Sandy.

So Pickett took them back to the Ogden and parked in her spot, then they walked down Fremont Street to the Golden Nugget. It was still a nice evening, but they both took jackets because they knew the walk back would be chilly.

Pickett felt frustrated by this entire thing. They had made a lot of progress in one day, going from a woman vanishing into a hotel room to understanding how she got out and that five women were doing this regularly.

But they had no idea why, or how to find the woman that for one year called herself Sandy.

The smell of pizza and prime rib in the buffet made Pickett realize just how hungry she was. It had only been four hours since lunch, but a draining four hours talking with the husband and old friend.

Robin wasn't there yet, so Sarge paid for all three of them since it was his turn. Since all three of them didn't have any issue with money, they had decided a few weeks back to just alternate paying for dinners and lunches. Just easier that way.

Then he and Pickett left their jackets at their normal table and went to get food.

Ten minutes later Robin joined them and within fifteen minutes they were all eating.

Pickett had gone for some prime rib, some breaded shrimp, and a pretty large salad with eggs. Sarge had his normal prime rib, ham, and potatoes. Robin always started with just a salad, fairly plain.

"So," Sarge said after a few minutes to Robin, "Any luck on trying to find out a connection between the five women?"

"Nothing yet," Robin said, shaking her head. "We are pretty convinced that this started for all of them in 1998. And that they were all in their early twenties. But their original identities seem to be very, very well hidden."

"So five women," Pickett said, "suddenly decide to become other women, marry or get into relationships, and then just vanish every year?"

"Pretty much," Robin said, finishing her salad and standing and heading for her main course.

"So back there in 1998 we have five women who knew each other," Sarge said, shaking his head as he cut at his prime rib, "suddenly vanish from their lives and start new lives, strings of new lives."

"Think we need to look for some event that had five friends involved?" Pickett asked. "Something that would have triggered whatever they are doing now."

"It would sure help if we could figure out why they were pulling the vanishing act every year," Sarge said.

Robin came back as they sat there eating and thinking. Around them the noise of the buffet felt like a welcoming background sound. There was just something about people laughing and enjoying themselves that made an atmosphere comfortable.

"I do have some news about the cleaning service," Robin said as she worked to put some sour cream on a baked potato. "There is no connection at all to any of the women and the company cleans all the time and has upwards of fifty hotels as clients. All their cleaners are from twenty to twenty-five. None older."

"Dead end," Sarge said.

"Completely," Robin said.

Pickett shook her head. "I would have lost that bet. I thought there was a chance the months of disappearances of the women matched the months of the cleaning for some reason."

Robin shook her head. "Nope. No connection anywhere. None of them ever worked for the company either."

Pickett felt disappointed in that. For some reason she was convinced the disappearances had to do with those return air ducts. No idea why she thought that, but she did.

"Any pattern to the months the five women disappear?" Sarge asked.

"Every other month for ten months," Robin said, "January, March, May, July, September. Same woman uses the same month every year."

"So we are past the last one," Pickett said.

Robin nodded. "Missing person's case on the last September one is still active but cold. As all eighty-five of the cases with these five women are."

"These five women's disappearing acts have sure been brutal to a lot of good people," Sarge said.

Pickett could tell he was really disgusted. She felt the same way.

FOURTEEN

November 16th, 2016
Las Vegas, Nevada

IT WASN'T UNTIL Sarge was working on a wonderful cheesecake that he remembered to ask if Robin had discovered when Sandy left the hotel.

"She didn't," Robin said. "I have one of Will's people going over facial recognition of all the security footage in the file one more time, but for three days after she vanished into that hotel, she did not leave. We're pretty sure of that."

Pickett had been sipping on a glass of wine and she looked startled. As startled as Sarge felt.

"She sure didn't stay in those return air ducts," Pickett said.

Sarge knew instantly what had happened. "Robin, is it still possible to get the room reservations from that hotel for that time?"

"Sure," Robin said, nodding. "You thinking she had a room for a few days?"

"Starting the day before," Pickett said. "I've been wondering how she would have gotten a change of clothes, new hair color, and so on. If she had a room booked the day before, she could have had clothes already there."

"And she would have been able to get into it easily through the return air system," Sarge said nodding.

Robin had out her notebook and was taking notes. "I'm thinking she would have stayed a full week. But this is going to be hard to narrow down."

"The names would be fake, more than likely a couple's name," Pickett said.

Sarge agreed. That was exactly what he was thinking.

"And if we can find that fake name, it might lead us to their next name," Robin said.

Both Sarge and Pickett shook their heads at that.

"I wouldn't expect that," Sarge said. "All signs are that these women are very, very careful and have been for a lot of years."

"Can't hurt to check, though," Pickett said.

"Agreed," Robin said. "So we have a pretty good idea how each woman vanishes now. But not one idea as to why."

"Or even who they are," Pickett said.

With that, they all sat in silence and then went back to working on their desserts.

Thirty minutes later Robin headed for home.

Sarge took Pickett's hand once they got out of the hotel and they headed up Fremont toward the Ogden condos. The air had a solid bite to it as he had expected and he was glad he had grabbed a jacket.

"Beautiful night," Pickett said as the strolled along once they got past the party atmosphere of the Fremont Street Experience.

Sarge had to agree. Even with the cold chill, the night was peaceful and the air clear and fresh.

"You up for a movie?" he asked after a half block. "Get our minds off of this crazy case."

"I'd love that," Pickett said, squeezing his hand.

When they reached the top floor of the Ogden, Pickett opened her door and he opened his, leaving it slightly open for her to follow in a few minutes. She needed to feed Nose her nightly treat and change her clothes. Pickett usually wore sweatpants and a sweatshirt around her condo and had started doing that when she came over.

Basically, he did the same.

He first gave Pete and Ree a snack and when they were munching away, he got out the popcorn machine and got it ready, then he went to change clothes. By the time he finished, Pickett and Nose were in the kitchen and she was picking up the cat dishes, rinsing them off, and putting them in the dishwasher.

The three kittens were already scampering off to play down the hallway toward the bedroom. He couldn't imagine living in this place without those kittens, now.

And living here without Pickett at his side.

As far as he was concerned, two retired detectives and three cats made a perfect family.

As the popcorn was starting, Pickett said, "Got a phone call from my friend Jean on my machine."

Sarge nodded. Pickett still had a home phone and all her friends had been trained to call her there for personal stuff.

"Jean said the secretary my ex left with has now left him."

Pickett was smiling and shaking her head.

Pickett's husband, about five years before, had left with his twenty-something secretary. That was why Pickett had enough money to buy the wonderful condo next door. Her settlement had been enough to buy the condo and have enough to live the rest of her life without even getting her retirement payments from the city.

Sarge and his former wife had parted on good terms about seven years before. Being a detective had basically killed that marriage, Sarge had no doubt.

"Think he's going to contact you?" Sarge asked.

Pickett just laughed. "Not a chance in hell. He always hated it when I was right and I got a hunch he's remembering my last words to him."

"And what were they?" Sarge asked, smiling.

"Nothing nasty," Pickett said. "I just told him to get as much as he could as often as he could from the young thing because it wasn't going to last."

Sarge laughed and Pickett just grinned.

"Karma is a bitch, isn't it?" Pickett said.

Sarge could only agree as three kittens streaked past the kitchen area, making enough noise to pretend to be a herd of elephants. Amazing that three creatures so small could make so much noise.

They even drowned out the popping corn.

PART THREE
Mucking the Hand

FIFTEEN

November 17th, 2016
Las Vegas, Nevada

PICKETT FINISHED HER omelet and sat back sipping on her morning coffee in the Golden Nugget Buffet. The normal customers and tourists were mostly on the other side of the restaurant, near the windows looking out over the pool area. The morning walk to breakfast had been chilly, but invigorating.

And the movie last night had been wonderful. They had decided to watch the original *Ghostbusters* movie, since when it first came out they had both been too busy with work to see it. It was wonderfully silly and just what she had needed.

And curling up next to Sarge and falling asleep with three kittens sleeping in different places around the bedroom had also been perfect as well. She wasn't sure how she had gotten so lucky to have him enter her life, but she was going to enjoy it as long as it lasted.

And he said he felt the same way.

Robin had met them for breakfast with a ton of reports she had generated last night, more than likely working while they were enjoying watching a giant marshmallow man roam the streets of New York.

Each report was the missing person's case on the women. All eighty-five times someone had cared enough to file a missing person's report. These five women had hurt a lot of people along the way with whatever they were doing.

Robin had then called each woman by the name of the month she vanished every year and done a summary of the jobs, traits, hair colors, looks, and so on for all five.

After Sarge finished looking at the last summary, Pickett asked, "Patterns at all that we could use to pinpoint who they are at the moment?"

"Nothing," Robin said. "All the changes seem to be random. Even the types of car they drive changes from incarnation to incarnation."

"They are all in their late thirties, now," Sarge said, "How are they aging?"

Robin dug through a file and pulled out pictures of all five from the last disappearance cycle. Pickett studied them. There was nothing at all outstanding about them. Attractive late-thirties women. Nothing more.

"The detectives on the last cycle of disappearances got DNA samples of the women from the last husbands and boyfriends and have them in the system," Robin said. "No hits at all as to history. But they are sisters."

"Sisters?" Pickett asked, shocked. She couldn't believe that all five were sisters.

Robin nodded. "Sisters. We are running DNA searches for any close or other family match in the system around the country, but that's going to take days. If not longer."

"But next time they vanish and the DNA is collected, it will hit," Sarge said.

Pickett nodded. "I'm betting they know that and don't care."

"Certainly won't help us find them now," Robin said.

"And the very first disappearances were as fake as all the others?" Sarge asked.

"They were," Robin said. "As best as we can find, all five sisters appeared out of the blue and got fake names and started into a new life."

"But why?" Sarge asked.

Robin only shrugged.

Pickett sipped on her coffee and Sarge leafed through the files as Robin went to get something more to eat.

The five women, five sisters, had to be doing this for a reason. And a carefully planned reason right from the start.

They weren't taking anything, they weren't actually hurting anyone in a criminal way. Pickett knew there wasn't a law saying it was against the law to run away from a life. So on the surface these women were doing nothing against the law.

On the surface.

But why would five sisters start down this road? None of this made any sense at all.

Pickett looked around at all the tourists enjoying their morning in the buffet. Maybe the view on this case was too narrow. People came into Las Vegas from all over the world. These five women had to have been from somewhere.

Robin put a plate of French toast in front of her chair and grabbed her napkin and sat down. As she bit into the toast, Pickett asked, "Where are these women from?"

"No idea," Robin said.

Sarge was looking at Pickett with his puzzled expression, so she went on.

"Is there a way to find out if say five sisters vanished somewhere in 1997 or 1998 at the same time?" Pickett asked. "All short, young women. Wouldn't that be in a file somewhere?"

Robin nodded, wiping off her hands and taking her pen and making a note. "Sure worth a computer search."

Sarge nodded, then suddenly grabbed the picture of Sandy Hunter at thirty-nine. "Computer search gave me an idea. You think these mid-to-late-thirties women might use a dating service to find the next husband?"

Pickett laughed and Robin again wiped off her hands from the syrup from her waffle and took notes.

"It will take some time to run facial recognition on the major dating sites around the time the women disappeared," Robin said. "But again, worth the search."

Pickett shook her head. "I doubt you will find anything. These women line up their next husbands a year ahead of leaving the last one."

"That's right," Sarge said.

"Still worth a search," Robin said.

"So you got some things to do," Pickett said to Robin. "Got any ideas about what we could do?"

"Ex-husbands," Robin said, sliding two folders toward Pickett. "Here is everything about March's last two husbands. Both of them are technically still married to her. Maybe one of them has something to add to this craziness."

"You thinking that after seventeen times," Sarge said, "Sandy Hunter, aka March, might be getting sloppy."

"One can only hope," Robin said.

Pickett could only agree to that statement. She had no doubt it was going to take some luck and more than likely a mistake one of the women made to break this open. And so far these five sisters didn't seem to be the types to make mistakes.

SIXTEEN

November 17th, 2016
Las Vegas, Nevada

ROBIN LEFT AND Sarge and Pickett sat and worked on their coffees while reviewing the files of the last two times Sandy Hunter had vanished. Two years ago her name had been Karen Dross and last year she had been named Kathy Charles.

They decided that they should talk to her husband Buddy Charles first, so Sarge got on the phone to the Detective Guy from the University Station who had caught the case. It was still an active case, so they needed to get the detective in charge permission to talk with Buddy Charles.

Detective Guy just laughed. "Be my guest. That case was cold from the first moment it hit my desk."

"Yeah, kind of like the one we're working," Sarge said. "Not sure if there's a connection, but we'll let you know if there is. Anything you can tell us about this Buddy Charles?"

"Nice guy, but really torn up that his new wife suddenly vanished. He's blaming himself even though he had absolutely nothing to do with it. Calling me every week for an update I just don't have."

"We'll see if we can talk him off the ledge a little," Sarge said. "Maybe give him some faith that the police are working on it."

"Thanks," Detective Guy said. "I think anything's going to help the guy."

Sarge hung up and looked at Pickett who had been listening.

"Put on your counselor hat," Sarge said. "We got a husband taking this really hard. And can't say as I blame him."

"Neither can I," Pickett said. "I wonder how many of the husbands didn't make it through this?"

Sarge just sort of shuddered and stood. "Not a question I want Robin looking into."

"Yeah, with that I agree."

It took them fifteen minutes to walk back to the Ogden as they had been doing every morning now for a month. Sarge loved the routine and the blocks of exercise. It wasn't much, but the walk to the casino and back every day made him feel like he was doing a little something.

Most days since he had met Pickett they had managed to spend a little time in the condo's exercise room. But he honestly liked walking more, especially walking with Pickett.

Pickett again drove. She liked to drive and it didn't stress her out and he didn't mind her driving in the slightest. In fact, he was pretty convinced she was a better driver than he was. So after just weeks of working together, they were already in a habit of her driving.

Pickett had called Buddy Charles at his work and asked if they could talk and he was more than welcoming. He was the CEO of a major grocery chain and they met him in his main store in his office suite. There was no doubt at all to Sarge that this guy had money.

He looked to be about forty, with a slight paunch and graying hair combed back. He stood about Sarge's height and seemed in shape. He had his suit jacket draped over the back of his desk chair and his tie loosened. The office was on the second floor and looked out at the Strip. A picture of his wife, Kathy, still occupied the corner of his desk.

Sarge and Pickett both identified themselves and showed their badges, then took seats in front of his large oak desk.

"So why more detectives on Kathy's disappearance?" Buddy said as they sat down. "Did something come up?"

"We're working all sorts of paths on this," Pickett said. "Detective Guy will call you at once if we have any leads?"

Buddy nodded and Sarge could see instantly what Detective Guy was talking about. This man was really, really depressed.

"We need to ask some personal questions about Kathy if you don't mind," Sarge said.

"Not at all," Buddy said. "Anything you think might help."

"When and how did you two meet?" Sarge asked.

"About two years ago now," Buddy said. "My first wife and I had divorced about five years ago and I was eating lunch at a little diner around the corner from here and she came in. We got

talking and ended up running into each other a few other times until I finally got up the nerve to ask her out in April. We were married four months later."

Sarge nodded and wrote all that down in his notebook. It fit the pattern of the women setting up the men while still with the previous husband.

"So before she vanished, did you sense anything was wrong?" Pickett asked.

"Nothing," Buddy said, shaking his head. "I thought we were happy. She sure seemed happy."

"Did she have any old friends?" Sarge asked. "Friends she traveled with?"

"Yeah," Buddy said. "Some old girlfriends back east. She got together with them twice while we were together."

"Did she say where?"

"She said she was going to Seattle in April, but turned out she went to San Francisco."

Sarge glanced at Pickett who suddenly sat forward.

"How did you know that?" Pickett asked.

"I had only known this woman for a month," Buddy said. "I got a lot of money and I would rather have that money go to my kids from my first wife than someone trying to take me. So I had her followed."

Sarge nodded. "Very smart. Did she meet some old friends?"

"She did," Buddy said. "Four other women around her age. They spent most of the time in a big suite in an older hotel there. Then she came home."

"She tell you about the change in plans?" Pickett asked.

"She did," Buddy said. "And I didn't even ask."

Sarge glanced at Pickett. The women knew they were being followed. And if Sarge was to bet, the hotel had return air ducts they could go in and out of in disguise.

But at least now they knew the five sisters got together for some reason twice a year. Still no idea why, but at least that was a start.

"Did you hire a professional to follow her?" Pickett asked.

Buddy nodded. "Sure did."

"You still have the report?"

Buddy shrugged and stood and went to a file cabinet built into one wall. He unlocked it and pulled out the report and handed it to Pickett. "You can keep it. Not doing me much good now at all."

"You hire a firm to try to find her?" Sarge asked.

Again Buddy nodded. "No damn luck. Last she was seen was going into the Benning Casino and Hotel. One of the other women from her job was supposed to meet her there in the café for lunch, but Kathy never showed in the restaurant. Just vanished into thin air. Her car was still in the basement parking garage."

Sarge knew exactly how she had vanished. She had found a camera dead area, put on a wig and a change of clothes, and then went into a guest room that was already reserved. But he didn't tell Buddy that. They just didn't dare yet.

"She took nothing?" Pickett asked.

"Her clothes she was wearing and the jewelry she had on. I had bought her a wonderful gold and diamond necklace and it was still in her jewelry box. She didn't take anything from me except my love and my pride."

"It isn't your fault, you know," Pickett said. "Things happen to good people."

"I know that here," Buddy said, pointing to his head. "But my gut and my heart tells me otherwise."

"Was it a happy year with her?" Sarge asked.

Buddy nodded.

"Then treasure that for the moment until we find out what happened. Sometimes a good year is a lot more than many couples get."

Buddy nodded and looked at the picture of Kathy on his desk. "I know that."

"You need to believe it," Pickett said.

"And that I'm still trying to do," Buddy said, staring at the picture.

All Sarge could do was sit there and be angry. Why in the world were these five sisters destroying so many men's lives?

They took nothing, but at the same time they took everything.

SEVENTEEN

November 17th, 2016
Las Vegas, Nevada

PICKETT AND SARGE walked out to her SUV in silence after leaving Buddy's office. Pickett just felt angry and she could tell that Sarge was as upset as she was.

She got into the car and they both just sat there in silence, letting the muffled traffic noise filter in. The day was starting to warm up a little, but not enough that she needed to turn on the air-conditioning. The sun actually felt good.

"On second thought," Sarge said, breaking the silence, "I think we need to get Robin and Will and their computers on finding out exactly what happened to these eighty-five men these women have destroyed."

"You think they are doing this on purpose?" Pickett asked, staring at the man she was quickly coming to love more than she wanted to admit.

"They are clearly doing this on purpose," Sarge said. "But if it's just for cover for something else, I don't know. But I do know they are heartless."

"With that I agree," Pickett said, taking out her cell phone and calling Robin. She quickly detailed out what they were looking for, then hung up.

"So let's take a look at the private-eye report," Sarge said.

Pickett opened the folder and leaned toward him, letting him see the basic contents. The first thing in the folder was a picture of the woman they were calling March, formally Sandy Hunter and four other women. This picture was labeled Kathy Charles. She was aging well from the pictures they had of her in the Sandy Hunter file. One of those women who didn't show many wrinkles and someone who had kept good care of herself.

The next picture was of the five sisters, all sitting around a restaurant table, eating. From the picture they seemed to be happy and enjoying themselves.

Pickett had no doubt it was the five women who kept vanishing every year.

"What happened that would cause these five sisters to dedicate seventeen years of their lives to meeting and leaving husbands?" Sarge asked, staring at the picture.

Pickett could only shake her head. Nothing at all made sense. Nothing. But something must have set the women on this course. Pickett and Sarge just needed to find out who the women had been originally and search their pasts, their real pasts for the clues.

They spent the next thirty minutes sitting in the car reading the private detective's report. Nothing at all new or unusual.

Pickett closed the file, then looked at Sarge. "Think this guy might give us some information not in the report?"

She pointed to the name on the report.

Some Classic Dean Wesley Smith Stories
Available at your favorite booksellers.

Sarge nodded. "He's the only one who has seen the five sisters together recently. Let's check him out with Robin and then ask Buddy to call the guy and tell him it would be all right to talk with us."

Pickett nodded. She agreed. There might be something.

She took out her phone and called Robin and put the phone on speaker.

"Anything?" Robin asked without saying hello.

"Not much from Charles," Pickett said, "but he had a private detective follow his soon-to-be wife on her meeting with her sisters."

"Did you get the report?" Robin asked, suddenly sounding excited. "And who was the agency?"

"Strickland Investigations," Pickett said. "H. Strickland was the guy who filed the report. Nothing in the report we didn't know."

"The guy is reputable," Robin said. "Will does work with him at times."

"We think it might not hurt to go talk with him," Pickett said. "See what is not in the report to the client. Would you set it up with him since Will knows him and we'll get permission from Buddy Charles to have him talk with us."

"Got it," Robin said. "And on the question about the husbands you asked earlier. All but two of them are still alive. One died of cancer, the other in a skiing accident. They all seemed to recover given time from their year with one of the sisters."

"Good," Sarge said, nodding.

Pickett felt relieved.

"I'll call you right back," Robin said, "as soon as I get in touch with Strickland."

Robin hung up and quickly dialed Buddy Charles.

Three minutes later they had Charles' permission to talk with his investigator

and Strickland would be waiting for them in his office.

A very busy morning so far. Pickett liked that. She just wished they were making progress toward the reason behind all this.

But as Sarge said as she started up the car to head for Strickland's office. "At least we have solved eighty-five missing persons' cold cases."

Normally, that would be really something. But something else was going on here besides five sisters unable to stay in relationships. She could just feel it.

EIGHTEEN

November 17th, 2016
Las Vegas, Nevada

SARGE HAD AN odd feeling about Henry Strickland from the moment they shook hands. Henry was a short man, not more than five-four, if that. He looked like any tourist visiting Las Vegas from the Midwest. His slightly graying hair was combed back, his loud Hawaiian shirt had more colors than the Vegas Strip, and he wore Bermuda shorts and white socks and black dress shoes.

Perfect Las Vegas tourist, even in November. Sarge would have walked past him without a second look.

Strickland's outer office was a sprawling modern complex with a dozen young people working computers, all dressed very casually. His office had a massive mahogany desk, windows that looked out over a golf course, and a bathroom off to one side that looked as modern as one of Sarge's bathrooms in his penthouse condo.

Clearly there was money in private investigation. Of course, Sarge knew that since Robin's husband Will was one of the richest people he had ever met and he did security and investigation as well.

Strickland pointed to two chairs in front of his desk and went around behind the desk to drop into a large, leather chair.

Pickett glanced back out the office window at all the people at the desks. "Can I ask what all those people are doing?"

"Background searches, mostly," Strickland said. "We hire out to churches, casinos, you name it, to do background searches on possible new employees."

Sarge nodded. That made complete sense. Someone had to do that sort of thing.

"So I got this call from Buddy Charles," Strickland said, leaning forward, "saying you two are looking into his wife's disappearance."

"His and others," Sarge said. "And he let us have your report about her trip to San Francisco, but we were wondering if there was more you didn't put in the report."

Strickland shrugged and opened a file in front of him on his desk. "I got this out when I heard you were coming and looked at it again. This is a duplicate of the file I gave Charles."

Sarge and Pickett both watched as Strickland looked quickly at the report, then nodded and closed it. "Only thing I didn't tell Buddy was that I was sure the five women knew that I was following them."

"We kind of figured as much," Pickett said. "When she told him about the new location."

Strickland nodded.

Sarge watched Strickland and he didn't seem at all surprised by that news.

"Let me tell you something else odd," Strickland said. "They spent most of their time in one suite. All of them had their own rooms, under varied names, but they also had a large suite that was separate. After they all headed to the airport I bribed a nice hotel maid to tell me what she had seen in that room. She said she had seen computers. Five computers set up around the suite."

Sarge sat back, surprised.

"Seriously?" Pickett asked.

"Big new Mac laptops," Strickland said, nodding. "The maid said she was hoping to save for one for her grandchild. I gave her a few hundred to help in the cause for her information."

"What would five sisters be doing with the laptops?" Pickett asked.

"Sisters?" Strickland asked, learning forward.

"Sisters," Sarge said.

He and Pickett and Robin had agreed on the way to see Strickland that he could be trusted and it wouldn't hurt to get his take on all of this. Since no crime had been committed that they knew about, letting Strickland into the investigation wouldn't hurt anything.

And besides, they figured they needed all the help they could get.

"Let me get you some more information," Pickett said, taking out her phone. "Robin and Will say you can be trusted, so we thought we would bring you completely into this to see if you have any ideas on just what in the world is going on."

"This is sounding stranger and stranger," Strickland said, smiling.

Sarge laughed. "You have no idea."

"Robin, please e-mail Mr. Strickland the photos we talked about and the page of details for each woman."

Pickett nodded, said thanks, and hung up.

Strickland had already turned and was bringing online his large desktop computer that sat to one side of his desk.

Sarge sat there, watching the investigator as he opened his e-mail and clicked on what Robin had sent him.

"Okay," Strickland said. "I'm seeing a picture of a lot of women. What is that all about?"

"Eighty-five of them," Sarge said. "All gone missing without a trace over the last seventeen years. Click on the next picture."

Strickland did and then sat back. "Are you telling me the same five women were those other eighty-five women?"

"They are all the same," Pickett said. "And we know from DNA from their last two disappearances that the five are all sisters."

"They meet a guy," Sarge said, "usually marry him, and then vanish without a trace, taking nothing but their clothes. No robbery, no reason, nothing."

"Exactly like Charles' wife did," Strickland said.

Sarge nodded. "That's why when we discovered you had actually seen all five together, we needed to bring you into this investigation."

Strickland nodded. "No idea who they are originally, I assume."

"Not yet," Pickett said. "We have an international search for anything family related on DNA. That's our best hope there."

"And no idea who they are with and what their names are now?"

"No idea," Sarge said. "Or if they are even continuing on. We are betting they are."

Strickland nodded. "I've trailed my fair share of women getting together for a few days of fun and friendship. These five felt different. They played all the parts, but they didn't seem to be really having fun. Just a gut thing."

"So this was some sort of planning meeting," Pickett said.

Sarge agreed. "And they meet like this twice a year."

"We need to figure out why and what they were doing on those computers," Strickland said.

Sarge just laughed. "That would sure help."

Strickland smiled. "I know a guy who just might be able to help us."

"Help us with what?" Pickett asked.

"Find out what those women were doing on those computers in that hotel," Strickland said.

"That was a year-and-a-half ago," Sarge said. "How would that be possible?"

Suddenly Pickett started laughing. She patted Sarge's arm. "He's talking about Mike Dans."

"Oh," Sarge said, shaking his head.

Strickland just smiled and said nothing, but it was clear Pickett was right. They were about to call the best computer expert in Las Vegas, the one who did things reputable agencies like Strickland's and Robin's husband couldn't do.

NINETEEN

November 17th, 2016
Las Vegas, Nevada

PICKETT REALLY LIKED and respected Mike Dans, even though she knew sometimes his methods didn't follow the strict letter of the law.

Mike and his girlfriend, Heather Voight, often worked with Julia and Lott and Andor on Cold Poker Gang cases. And Mike really enjoyed helping out the Cold Poker Gang as much as possible.

Sarge said he had met Mike on a robbery case about ten years before and liked him. Mike was a former Special Forces guy who hadn't lost a step or a bit of muscle. He kept his hair short and had an infectious smile that hid a brilliant mind.

He also controlled a small army of Special Forces retired soldiers for all sorts of jobs, many off the books. It was that group of highly-trained men that had rescued hundreds of prisoners from tunnels under Las Vegas just a month ago. Mike and his people took no credit or payment. They had just done what they had needed to do.

Mike had done Sarge favors at times over the years and Pickett knew that Sarge had done a few in return. Mike ran a security firm, only not a famous one like Robin's husband's firm, but a firm that stayed behind the scenes.

Mike and his people were also experts in all sorts of computer issues. And Mike was the best of them all.

Pickett knew that Mike's firm worked for Will at times, and it didn't surprise her that he also worked for Strickland's firm when needed.

They decided that Sarge should call Mike, since that would help Strickland keep his hands clean a little more. So as Sarge dialed Mike's number, Strickland excused himself to use the restroom.

From Sarge's side of the conversation that Pickett could hear, Mike seemed happy to hear from them. They hadn't talked with Mike since the amazing work that he and his team did a month ago.

"So," Sarge said after a few moments of talking with Mike, "we have found ourselves in another strange case."

Sarge laughed and nodded. "Yeah, seems we attract them. Right now I am sitting in Henry Strickland's office with Pickett. Henry has excused himself to go use the restroom while I talk with you. The reason I am calling is that we could sure use some help."

Pickett watched as Sarge nodded. "Here is what we need. In April of 2015, five women stayed in a high-end hotel in San Francisco. They each had their own room, but they also rented a suite where they worked for three days on computers. Any chance we could figure out anything about what they were doing?"

Sarge nodded, then said, "Worth a try. At this point anything will help. I'll have Strickland send you the entire file, since he did surveillance on the five women."

"Thanks, Mike," Sarge said. "Make sure you charge me for your time on this. Full rate."

Sarge laughed and then hung up.

Pickett smiled. "I'm betting he said his full rate was lunch, right?"

"Right," Sarge said.

At that moment Strickland came out of the bathroom. "I keep telling him he works too cheap."

Strickland sat down at his computer and two minutes later turned away. "Mike's got the entire report. Now, explain to me how you got started on all this."

Pickett laughed and for the next fifteen minutes they filled Strickland in completely on the cold case of Sandy Hunter that opened this can of worms and how she got out of the hotel room and so on.

All Strickland did was sit, looking stunned, with his mouth open slightly.

Pickett knew that feeling. This case tended to do that to people.

PART FOUR
Drawing a Dead Hand

TWENTY

November 17th, 2016
Las Vegas, Nevada

SARGE SIPPED AT the iced tea the waitress at the Bellagio Café had brought him. It tasted great after a morning of interviews and no real progress. Strickland had helped some in making this a focus and had got the information to Mike Dans that Mike would need to have any hope of doing any tracing.

On the way to lunch from Strickland's office, Pickett had explained to Sarge how it might be possible for Mike to find out some information about what those women were doing, even a year-and-a-half later. It was going to depend on how the hotel internet connections worked and if they stored usage data on the cloud.

Sarge took away from what Pickett said that what Mike was doing was a long shot, but worth the try.

Pickett hung up her cell and also sipped her iced tea.

"Robin is about ten minutes out," Pickett said. "She wants us to order her normal for her if she isn't here by the time the waitress comes back."

Sarge nodded. Frighteningly enough, the three of them had normal meals they ate regularly when working a case like this. He wondered if that had anything to do with their age or if it was just what he had always done. He honestly had no memory of that, but if he had to guess, he would guess it was set-in-our-ways age.

"So," Sarge said, smiling at the wonderful woman beside him, "We have made a lot of headway to go nowhere real."

"We solved all the missing person's cold cases," Pickett said. "That's something. Might be a record for the most cases closed at once. And we know they are all alive."

"But alive where?" Sarge asked.

"I'm betting right here," Pickett said, shrugging, "all married or getting married, setting up husbands number eighteen."

They sat for a moment in silence, then Pickett said, "You think at some point we might move in together?"

Sarge laughed and looked at the woman he had fallen in love with.

"So why did this topic come up now?"

"Just thinking of those five women rushing into marriage," Pickett said, "for clearly the wrong reason, whatever it may be, and that got me wondering about our two condos and our situation."

"You want an honest answer or my safe answer," Sarge asked, smiling.

She laughed. "I want both. First the safe answer."

Sarge nodded. "Safe answer would be I think given time I would hope it would happen."

"Honest answer now," Pickett said.

"I would love to move in with you or you move in with me tomorrow. And besides, the kids would love it as well."

He was surprised that he didn't feel the slightest bit worried about admitting that to her.

She smiled and leaned over and kissed him. "I agree. And I had a thought if we can get the building management to sign off."

"Listening," he said.

"We put in an archway with pocket doors between our two places," she said. "We can leave the doors open most of the time, but if we have guests, we can close the door and let them use my place. And if we ever have to sell one place or the other, we just close it back up."

"Oh, god," Sarge said, smiling. "We're going to have guests all the time."

"So you like the idea?" Pickett asked.

"I like it a lot," Sarge said.

"Like what?" Robin said, sliding into the booth across from Sarge and next to Pickett. Neither of them had seen her coming across the restaurant.

"Some condo ideas," Pickett said. "We'll tell you later."

At that moment the waitress also appeared and took their orders for lunch. After she left, Robin said, "I have some news."

Sarge was stunned at that. Even though they were moving fast on this case, it felt to him as if they had hit the spot where the case would go cold again.

"What?" Pickett asked.

"We found who these sisters were originally," Robin said.

She opened a notebook and started reading. "We got a hit on the DNA from a distant family member and were able to track to the five sisters. Their original name was Jones."

"Jones?" Sarge asked, trying not to laugh. "Five women who change their names every year were originally Jones?"

Robin nodded. "Our March woman is the oldest at forty. Her original name was Beverly Jones. Then there were two sets of twins, not identical. So they are all within three years of the same age."

"Wow," Pickett said.

"Here is what gets interesting," Robin said. "When Beverly was fourteen, their father killed their mother. Seems he had been beating on the mother and the girls for years. Finally went too far."

Sarge felt his stomach twist. Now they were getting a glimpse of maybe why these women didn't stay with their husbands, but from all of the reports, the husbands were good men.

"What happened to the girls?" Pickett asked.

"Father went to jail, died there a year later in a knife fight," Robin said. "The girls were split up and put into foster care since they had no real other family that could deal with five kids."

"Oh, shit," Pickett said.

Sarge felt the same way.

Robin just nodded. "Five abused sisters split apart and put into a child care system. What possibly could go wrong with that?"

Sarge just shook his head.

"Beverly kept them all in touch," Robins said, "and together as much as possible, from the reports we found. When the last set of twins aged out, the five girls vanished. They never talked to even distant family members again."

The three of them sat there in silence for a moment, the sounds of the restaurant and the distant casino background noise.

The five sisters had lived through a nightmare made worse by no relatives being able to take them in. They had stuck together to get through it, which made sense to Sarge. But so many other things still made no sense at all.

Finally Sarge asked. "So why would that background, that history, that tragedy, make these women marry and then leave a husband, seemingly good husbands, every year?"

Neither Pickett nor Robin had an answer for that question.

The more they learned about all this, the more puzzling it became.

TWENTY-ONE

November 17th, 2016
Las Vegas, Nevada

THEY ATE LUNCH while bouncing questions around about the motives of the five sisters, finding none at all that made any sense to Pickett. What had happened to those young girls, the horror they had survived, would certainly scare anyone.

And it made sense they were still very tight and had disappeared from any contact with a family that had allowed that horror to continue. But vanishing every year from good spouses just made no sense.

As they were just finishing their meals, Sarge's phone rang and he answered it. After a moment he said, "Hi, Mike. Any luck?"

As Sarge spoke and Pickett and Robin watched, Sarge got out his small notebook from his shirt pocket and started to write.

Pickett wanted to lean over and see what he was writing, but instead just sat there.

Finally, Sarge said, "Thanks, Mike. We owe you."

Mike must have said something because Sarge laughed before hanging up.

"Mike was able to get into the hotel servers and cloud storage," Sarge said, "but you didn't hear me say that."

Both other cops nodded and smiled. This would have been another matter if they were all still officially on the force, but they were just mostly private citizens who could bend rules far more than regular detectives could do.

"He said the hotel doesn't record exact connections or things like that, but they store usage from each room and basic levels for three years."

"Makes sense for lawsuit reasons," Robin said.

Sarge nodded. "Mike said he couldn't dig out specific addresses or anything like that," Sarge said, "but the activity from that room showed all five were online most of each day on the five computers. He said their activity looked like they were searching all sorts of databases."

"Searching for what?" Robin asked a half second before Pickett could ask the same question.

"Mike was wondering the same thing," Sarge said, shaking his head.

They sat there for a moment. Pickett knew they needed to get focused again. Somehow.

"Okay," Pickett said. "We have solved a bunch of missing person cold cases."

"And a few active ones," Sarge said.

"So we could quit right now," Pickett said, "get this to one of the active duty detectives and get him to get it in the papers to flush out the five women."

She hated that idea, but she wanted to float it to Sarge and Robin. Both of them were shaking their heads.

"So why are we not calling this one closed?" Pickett asked. "For me it is a gut sense that something bigger is going on."

"Agree," Sarge said, nodding.

"Completely," Robin said.

"So," Pickett said, "we need to change this focus to a conspiracy focus. We don't know the crime, but we know something is happening."

Both Sarge and Robin nodded.

The part that was bothering Pickett the most was that these women actually hadn't committed any real crime. At least that they could find.

"So," Sarge said, "with that focus, what about tracing how those fake ids and backgrounds are done."

"Will has two people on that," Robin said, nodding. "It bothers him that these five sisters could have such perfect and deep backgrounds for fake names year after year. That takes work, time, and preparation and it is driving Will nuts."

Pickett was very glad to hear that. When Will got focused, he found things that no one else seemed to be able to find.

"Good," Sarge said. "So everything keeps twisting around to their motive for pulling these vanishing acts."

"We have three theories," Pickett said. "Cover for a crime is the first. A lack of ability to commit to one relationship is second. A giant game is third. And the more I learn about these women, the more I think the first one is the only logical conclusion."

Again, both Sarge and Robin agreed.

The sounds of the distant casino filled the quiet in the booth. Finally Pickett asked, "Anyone got any ideas?"

Sarge nodded. "It's a long shot, but I think we get permission from the active detectives to tell Rich Hunter and Buddy Charles who his wife really was, her background, what happened to her, what she was doing."

Pickett stared at Sarge. "You think them knowing who she was and her background might put a puzzle piece into this mess?"

Sarge smiled. "As I said, it's a long shot, but damned if I can think of anything else to do this afternoon."

Pickett could only nod to that because she didn't have any better idea either.

TWENTY-TWO

November 17th, 2016
Las Vegas, Nevada

ROBIN LEFT TO go back to help Will on his searches. Sarge and Pickett got their iced teas refilled and stayed in the booth, working together on a piece of key lime pie. From there they called Detectives Bower and Guy and told them what they had discovered so far and asked them to keep quiet on it for the moment, since they were working something bigger. They asked for permission to go talk with the two husbands again.

Both detectives agreed, as Sarge knew they would.

Pickett called Rich Hunter and he was surprised, but agreed to once again meet them in his office in forty minutes.

Buddy Charles said he would be open at 4 p.m. which gave them more than two hours to talk with Rich.

Sarge had no doubt at all that this would prove pointless and difficult to say to both husbands. But someone had to do it, so they might as well be the ones giving the news to the two men they had talked to.

Pickett paid the bill and thirty minutes later Sarge held the heavy door of the old office building on campus open for her.

"Always a gentleman," she said, smiling at him.

"Old school," he said.

She smiled at him. "We'll see how old later tonight."

All he could do was smile and hope he didn't blush at where his imagination went immediately.

Rich Hunter was behind his desk when they got to his open door. He signaled they should come in and have a seat and close the door, which Sarge did.

"So twice in two days," Rich said, "after all these years. Have you discovered what happened to Sandy?"

"We have," Pickett said.

Rich actually sat forward, stunned at that. "You know what happened to her? Is she dead?"

"No," Sarge said, "she is very much alive."

With that Rich sat back in his chair, the look of shock on his face clear.

Sarge figured the only way to get this out clearly was to start from the beginning.

"Sandy's real name was Beverly Jones," Sarge said. "She is the oldest of five sisters from back east. From the best we can figure, she was married three times before she met you, staying in each relationship about one year."

Rich started to object and Sarge held up his hand to stop him.

"We know how insane this sounds, but hear us out," Sarge said. "From 1998 to this year, Beverly Jones married and then vanished seventeen times. Her four sisters did the same thing."

Rich was shaking his head slowly from side to side.

"The five sisters grew up in a very abusive home," Pickett said. "When Beverly was fourteen, their father basically beat their mother to death. Beverly held the sisters together while they were all in foster care until they all vanished without a trace when the youngest two turned eighteen. Two years later in 1998 they started their vanishing routine here in Las Vegas."

"But why?" Rich asked, his voice not much more than a whisper. "She didn't take anything from me. Nothing. The police checked and we didn't have much to take as it was."

"Why is what we are trying to figure out," Pickett said.

Now Available
from all your favorite booksellers
in trade paper and electronic editions.

Sarge just watched Rich's reaction. It was as he had suspected it would be. Stunned. Sarge had no doubt anger would come soon enough.

"Did Beverly, I mean Sandy say anything about children's homes?" Sarge asked. "Or about abusive relationships, sisters, anything that you can remember?"

"No," Rich said, shaking his head slowly. "She seemed so happy. Never said anything about sisters or abusive men or anything. She didn't even seem to mind my cousin Karl who treated his wife like shit. It didn't seem to bother her the few times we were around him."

"What happened to Karl?" Pickett asked a fraction of a second before Sarge could.

"Died just after Sandy vanished," Rich said. "But I was so focused on finding Sandy, I didn't even bother to go to the funeral."

Sarge glanced at Pickett, then asked Rich, "How did Karl die?"

"Food poisoning of some sort," Rich said, shrugging. "Or drank himself to death. I don't think anyone on the planet missed him, including his wife."

Pickett nodded.

Sarge wasn't sure what they had just discovered, but he had a hunch it might go deeper.

"Rich," Sarge said, "Other than your wife, can you please keep this to yourself for a few more days?"

"I can do that," Rich said, nodding. "You trying to figure out why she did this?"

"We are," Pickett said as she and Sarge stood.

Rich stood as well. "Is what she did to me and the other men illegal?"

"No," Sarge said. "But trust me, we will make her pay if we can."

Pickett reached out and shook Rich's hand. "Thanks for your help and sorry for the bad news."

"You figured out what happened to her," Rich said. "After this long, that's actually good news."

Sarge shook his hand as well. "Detective Bower will be in touch when it is all right to tell more people than your wife."

"Thank you," Rich said.

Sarge had a hunch that Buddy Charles, the next husband they planned on telling, wasn't going to take the news as well.

TWENTY-THREE

November 17th, 2016
Las Vegas, Nevada

WHEN THEY GOT back to the car, Pickett called Robin, put the call on speakerphone, and told her about the abusive cousin dying right after Beverly vanished.

Robin said, "Holy shit. We'll get right on it."

And then hung up.

Pickett and Sarge both laughed.

"I love it when she does that," Pickett said. "Means she is excited."

Pickett knew that was going to be a tough search, through eighty-five husbands' extended families to find abusive men. But there was no doubt Robin and Will and his people could do it and do it quickly.

As Pickett headed them to Buddy Charles' office, she couldn't help but think that maybe, just maybe they had found the reason behind all of this.

They had just pulled up into the parking lot of Buddy's store and main office complex when Robin called back.

Pickett put it on speakerphone and Robin instantly started talking.

"Every husband's family we have checked so far, and that's twenty, had an abusive male die right after the fake wife disappeared. All of them, in one form or another, from food poisoning. Ten of them actually died in the hotel the woman vanished into."

"No one put any of this together?" Sarge asked.

Pickett felt the same sort of shock that Sarge had in his voice.

"Seems there was no need to," Robin said. "No one before us put these women together to see this kind of pattern, remember."

Pickett nodded on that.

"Think we need to talk with Buddy?" Sarge asked.

"Not yet," Robin said. "Head for home and I'll call you in an hour or so when we get the full picture in place."

"Oh, thank god," Sarge said.

Pickett laughed. "Yeah, not looking forward to this conversation."

And she hadn't been. She wanted to leave that to the active detectives on the case.

"When you cancel, tell him we are making progress and we'll be in touch," Robin said. "And I'll call you in an hour or so."

With that she hung up.

"Looks like we might have caught a break," Sarge said.

Pickett could only agree with that. She listened while Sarge thanked Buddy Charles for making time for them but they had to chase a lead and would be back with him as soon as things worked out.

Then Pickett got them through the later afternoon traffic and into her parking spot at the Ogden. On the way they had both decided they needed a little exercise, so they met fifteen minutes later in the condo's exercise room. No one else was there and they both did thirty minutes of running and weights before heading back upstairs for showers.

They were in Sarge's condo, feeding all three kittens their evening treat together when Robin called back.

Again Pickett put the phone on speaker.

"Every husband had an abusive family member that died right after the disappearance of the wife," Robin said. "All of them, no exceptions, and all from a form of food poisoning or alcohol poisoning."

"Any of them found to be an actual poison?"

"One doctor thinks that two of the men were killed purposely and both cases remain open as possible murders," Robin said. "In both cases both men showed up at the hospital in cabs, extremely sick and died within days without regaining consciousness. Cab drivers said the men were picked up at two of the hotels our women disappear into."

Pickett was shocked.

Could this actually be possible? Could these five sisters be serial killers and damn good ones.

"How long after the women disappeared," Sarge asked, "were the two possible murders committed?"

"One was six days," Robin said. "One was eight days."

"Any idea what the poison was?" Pickett asked.

"The doctor on the two cases think it was Croton Oil." Robin said. "It is used in animal lab testing in pain experiments and can be made from seeds of the Croton Tigium plant that grows in this area of the country."

"Mimics food poisoning?" Sarge asked.

"Almost impossible to spot and only takes ten to twenty drops to be fatal," Robin said. "You can add it to drinks or food and it takes about fifteen minutes for the reaction to hit once the poison is ingested."

"So they don't need a lot of it," Pickett said.

"Exactly," Robin said. "If what I have learned is right, the five women have killed eighty-five abusive men."

"Revenge for what their father did to their mother," Sarge said.

Pickett agreed completely.

"We now have a motive and a crime," Pickett said. "But no way to prove any of it and no idea where the women are now."

"Yeah, there's that," Robin said.

"Well, this is progress," Sarge said.

Pickett nodded. It was movement forward and smack into another dead end.

"You two enjoy your evening. Will and I are going to have date night. And no, don't ask."

With that Robin hung up.

Pickett laughed and at that moment the three kittens all ran into the living room together. Kittens seemed to never do anything slow.

And they were sure a wonderful distraction from the ugliness of the world.

PART FIVE
Still Another Dead Hand

TWENTY-FOUR

November 20th, 2016
Las Vegas, Nevada

SARGE WAS ABOUT as discouraged as he got on a case. For three days they had covered everything they could think of.

Nothing.

No headway at all.

As more and more information about the deaths came in, there was little doubt the men they were targeting were abusers. Clearly the five sisters did their research, which was more than likely what they were doing in those retreat hotel rooms.

And they did their research by marrying into a family to get the inside information about the abuser. Very careful as to their targets.

And from what Pickett and Sarge could figure talking to husbands, the sisters did it without much attention. For every husband they had talked to in three days, it was clear that at one point or another the sisters met each victim.

Today, Sarge and Pickett and Robin had all decided on trying to figure out how the sisters got the poison into the abuser's drinks or food.

It was a wonderful Sunday in late November, just four days before Thanksgiving, and Sarge wondered if he and Pickett had even needed the light jackets they wore on their walk to the Golden Nugget buffet. The sun was low, but had some warmth to it and the air felt like it might actually warm up.

Sunday in Vegas was like most other days in Vegas to Sarge. Neither he nor Pickett were religious, and besides, as a detective, cases didn't follow weekend rules, which had been part of the problem with his marriage.

Actually, the only way anyone who didn't work a regular five-day-a-week job in Vegas could tell any difference was that on Friday and Saturday nights there were a few more people than other nights. And on Sunday morning people in the casinos were either hung over or desperate to try their luck one more time before climbing on their plane home.

And most of them were dragging luggage around.

The buffet wasn't even half full and no family or hungover gamblers were near Sarge and Pickett's normal table when they got there. Robin hadn't arrived yet, so they got coffee ordered for all three and put their jackets at the table and headed to get food.

Robin arrived ten minutes later and within fifteen minutes all three of them were eating.

Sarge hadn't realized just how hungry he was this morning. He and Pickett had stayed up late watching a Mission Impossible movie. Nothing like watching a movie with fresh popcorn, three kittens,

and the woman he loved to make a perfect Saturday night.

"Notebooks," Robin said as she finished her slice of ham and pulled out her spiral notebook.

Sarge took out his small pocket notebook and put it beside his plate, then went back to finishing his second waffle. Robin's call for notebooks meant they needed to talk about the case.

"I don't know if it's going to help us at all on this," Robin said, "but we need to focus on how the poison is being delivered. So I have all eighty-five case files of each death."

She took out of her pack a pile of gray folders and set them on an open area on the table.

To Sarge, the files were small. He was used to murder files and only two of these were even being investigated as possible murders. Those two files were on top and were the thickest. The rest were thin.

Very thin. Just unusual deaths in hotels or from food poisoning of undetermined origin.

The folders were so thin that Robin could pick all of them together out of her pack without a problem.

"I did a bunch of research on Croton Oil," Robin said. "It's frighteningly quick and lethal. It has to be ingested to do any real harm. And it causes extreme pain, so much so that the victims tend to drop into comas before eventually dying."

"So they have no time to talk," Pickett said, which was exactly what Sarge had been thinking.

"No time," Robin said, nodding.

"How hard would it be to get?" Pickett asked.

Robin shrugged. "Not difficult in enough quantity to kill this many men. A small jar would do it and the stuff isn't regulated."

"Oh," Pickett said, scratching something off her notebook.

"So connections in the deaths to the three hotels the women use?" Sarge asked.

"Half of the men were found dead in the three hotels," Robin said. "Another dozen or so managed to get either into cabs or to hospitals before collapsing. Cab records show they all came from the three hotels."

"The rest?" Pickett asked.

Robin shrugged and pointed to the files. "No mention at all. Three collapsed on the sidewalk, the rest died in the hospital without any record of how they got there."

"So let's just assume all of them were poisoned in the three hotels," Sarge said. "Safe assumption?"

"Seems very safe," Robin said, nodding.

"And the women can get in and out of any room in the hotel at will," Pickett said. "So they vanish into the hotel, change identity, stay under a fake name in another room until the target gets brought to the hotel and then manage to get the target poisoned, usually in a room."

"This has to be simple," Sarge said, sitting back and thinking about it. "Eighty-five times this has happened, so the method of getting the poison into the food has to be simple and not involve anyone else."

Both Pickett and Robin nodded, clearly also thinking.

Sarge then realized what he had said. "Not involve anyone else but the sisters."

Robin sat forward and started making notes.

"You thinking another sister lured each man into the hotel?" Pickett asked.

"They can't trust another person," Sarge said, "and the men need to get there in some fashion or another. How about in the two cases being looked at as a murder, any link to a woman?"

Robin slid him one file and Pickett another. In the file Sarge had, it was clear that there was no mention of anyone with the victim and the hotel room was under the victim's name.

"Witness in this one saw the victim with a woman in the hotel," Pickett said. "Short, in good shape, long blonde hair."

"Short," Sarge said, nodding.

"Robin," "Pickett said, "any chance we can get security video of this man and the woman entering the hotel?"

"We can," Robin said, nodding, gabbing her phone. "I'll get someone on it with facial recognition. But I am betting Sarge is right on this."

"So am I," Pickett said.

Sarge just smiled as Robin talked to someone in Will's office, then hung up.

"We'll know in fifteen minutes," Robin said.

Sarge wasn't so sure it was going to get them any closer to the five sisters, but in three days it was the first forward progress they had made and that felt great.

TWENTY-FIVE

November 20th, 2016
Las Vegas, Nevada

AROUND THEM THE buffet sounds were quieting down as more and more of the morning breakfast crowd left. Now it was mostly just the sounds coming from the kitchen area that echoed over the large space. Pickett really felt comfortable here and she liked how the staff mostly just left them alone to take care of themselves, except to swoop past to pick up dirty plates and refill coffee.

Pickett felt slightly excited that they had had a breakthrough. It wasn't confirmed yet, but she was sure that Sarge was right and that the sisters helped each other.

And it made sense that there would be two of them in case something went wrong. After all, they were luring abusive men into hotel rooms to be alone. It wouldn't have surprised Pickett if a third sister was also in the return air ducts waiting to help.

"So if another of the sisters in disguise help get the man into the hotel room," Sarge said, "that brings us back to how in the world are they getting these disguises and identifications?"

That question had bothered Pickett a great deal.

Robin nodded. "Will asked the same question again last night. He has had no luck at all with the answer. These women set up complete fake histories and they manage to get driver's licenses and birth certificates. Very, very professional and all the identification and fake history holds up to a pretty good background check."

"Any sign they take the id from someone else?" Pickett asked.

"No," Robin said. "They make these new identities up out of whole cloth."

"How?" Sarge asked. "If they are going under fake identities into these hotels with the men, those have to be solid ids in case something goes wrong. So they could be coming up with upwards of ten completely new identities every year for the last seventeen years."

"Patterns in the identities?" Pickett asked.

Robin nodded and wrote in her notebook. "Might be worth a shot at running a computer program over the fake identities we know to see if there are repeating patterns of backgrounds, jobs, hometowns, and so on."

"And money?" Sarge said. "None of this can be cheap and they seem to take nothing from their husbands."

Money was something Pickett hadn't thought of at all.

"Damn," Robin said, looking up. "Each identity had to open a bank account of some sort and transfer money or write a check. That might be a link."

Pickett watched as Robin went back to quickly writing in her notebook.

Sarge excused himself to go get some dessert and Pickett asked him to bring her a piece of cherry pie if there was any.

Robin kept writing and Pickett just sat thinking. There had to be a way into the covers that these five women had set up. Since it was November, the women were more than likely working on their next husbands, maybe getting married by now. More than likely the woman who had been Sandy Hunter was already married or close.

They had to figure out how to find these five women, even if at the moment they couldn't pin anything on them.

Suddenly Pickett realized what she had been thinking about.

Marriage.

There were a lot of marriages in Las Vegas every year. Hundreds a day. But they had these women's sizes and general ages.

Sarge slid a piece of cherry pie in front of her and sat down with a piece of his own.

"Robin," Pickett said.

Robin glanced up at Pickett, looking suddenly worried. Pickett never just called her by name like that unless it was something important and Robin knew it.

"I know after the case a month ago, none of us want to think about marriage stuff," Pickett said.

Sarge had a piece of pie halfway to his mouth. He stopped and put the piece down on his plate.

"Somewhere right about now the January and March sister and maybe the May sister might be getting a marriage license."

Robin nodded, thinking. Then she said, "We have their ages. If we could get the files, we could sort for age."

"Mike can get us the files again," Sarge said.

Pickett nodded. It was Mike in the big tunnel case last month who had helped them find key evidence by hacking into the marriage license database.

"How were all of the women married before?" Pickett asked. "Chapels, churches, backyards?"

"Nothing at all in any of the files on that," Robin said. "But we can look that up easily since all the wedding licenses had to be filed after the ceremony to make the marriage valid. All that is public."

She wrote a quick note in her book, closed it, gathered up the files, and put them in her pack and stood. "Will and I have a ton of searches to do and he's going to want to bring in extra help on this. If they get married in chapels, the photos will be available."

At that moment her phone rang and she answered it. She nodded for a moment, then said, "Thank you."

She put her phone away and looked at Sarge and Pickett.

"The woman seen with the last victim from September going into the hotel was Miss March. She had on a brown-haired wig, had heels that made her seem taller, and wore dark glasses. But facial has it at a one hundred percent match."

"So she lured Miss September's victim into the hotel," Sarge said.

"And one of them poisoned him," Pickett said. She could feel her stomach twisting.

"We have got to find these women before January," Sarge said.

"We don't have them rounded up by early December," Robin said, "we go public with all this. Splash their photos over the news and papers. We'll lose them, but save five lives."

Pickett could only nod to that. She didn't want to have these women vanish. She wanted to arrest them.

Personally.

TWENTY-SIX

November 20th, 2016
Las Vegas, Nevada

AFTER ROBIN LEFT, Sarge called Mike Dans again and asked for the favor of hacking the marriage licenses. Sarge couldn't believe he was asking someone to break the law. He never would have done that as an actual detective, but retired now, sometimes small lapses over the line saved lives.

Mike agreed and then Sarge and Pickett finished their cherry pies and sipped on their coffee.

"Seems like we made a little progress again this morning," Pickett said.

"It does," Sarge said.

"But something is bothering you, isn't it?"

Sarge glanced at Pickett and smiled. He loved how she could already read him.

Before meeting her, having someone be able to really see him would have bothered him something awful. But he really liked it with Pickett.

"I've just been worrying about the evidence," Sarge said. "Even if we track and find these women, it will be like catching an endangered trout. Catch and release."

Pickett nodded and sipped on her coffee as a waitress nearby worked on cleaning all the empty tables.

"I think as we work on finding these five women," Sarge said, "we also need to start building a real case against them."

"And how do we start that?" Pickett asked.

"The poison is one lead," Sarge said. "I had never even heard of Croton Oil before this case."

"Neither had I," Pickett said. "We could also get them on creating fake ids and polygamy to hold them. Those we might be able to prove."

Sarge agreed with that. His focus was the murders, but at least they had something they might be able to hold the sisters on. But both of those charges wouldn't hold them for long. Days, maybe. And then the sisters would vanish.

"Also they all took their diamond wedding or engagement rings," Pickett said. "The most recent ones we could hold on felony theft."

Sarge nodded to that. It would be enough to hold them for a time. But they had to prove conspiracy on at least one or two of the murders.

Somehow.

If they could find them first.

They headed back to the Ogden at a comfortable walk. Sarge was really enjoying the cool morning air and being with Pickett, but he just couldn't get his mind off of one element of this case.

The money.

Finally, he decided that he needed to talk about what he was thinking about.

"I'm bothered by the money on all this," Sarge said.

"So am I," Pickett said, smiling. "In fact, that was what I was thinking about."

Sarge laughed and squeezed her hand.

"So let me outline what has me the most worried on this about the money," Pickett said.

"Fire away," Sarge said. "I bet we're on the same track."

"The women leave everything behind," Pickett said. "They are going to need a brand new wardrobe, hairstyle, everything. And that's not cheap, let me tell you."

Sarge nodded. "I honestly hadn't thought of that. I was thinking about a new apartment, first and last month's rent, new furniture to look the part they were playing, and so on."

"And they would already have much of that set up ahead of leaving," Pickett said. "Not only are these women masters of disguises, but in banking and setting up fake bank identities as well."

"Cars," Sarge said. "The sisters are buying five cars a year as well."

"This is really adding up," Pickett said as they reached the ground floor of the Ogden building. "And over seventeen years, where is the money coming from?"

"We're missing something," Sarge said. "I can feel it but darned if I can put my finger on it. And it has to do with the money."

"How about we go up to the rooftop balcony in your place," Pickett said, "get a couple cups of fresh coffee and sit with our notebooks staring out over the city."

"A perfect way to spend a Sunday morning in my opinion," Sarge said.

And it was.

But in two hours and three cups of coffee, they made no progress at all. But Sarge didn't mind, actually. Sitting with Pickett and staring over the wonderful view was reward enough.

TWENTY-SEVEN

November 20th, 2016
Las Vegas, Nevada

SARGE MADE THEM a light sandwich for lunch and after lunch they decided they both needed some exercise. For Pickett, that was the best way to clear her brain.

So after forty minutes of weights and running, she was back in her shower when one thought sort of came at her out of the blue.

What happens if the sisters weren't the only ones?

Pickett quickly got dressed and headed over to Sarge's place. He was out of the shower, but still getting dressed. He looked up at her and smiled when she came into his bedroom.

Damn, he was the most handsome man she could ever imagine being in love with. His muscles were still toned, his hair a gray that made him look distinguished, and his smile when he looked at her told her just exactly how lucky she was.

"Had this really horrid thought," she said as Sarge went back to putting on his shoes. "What happens if the sisters aren't the only ones doing this sort of thing?"

Sarge looked up at her, clearly shocked and a little puzzled.

"What are you thinking?"

"I honestly don't know," Pickett said. "As far as we can tell, these five sisters arrived in Vegas young and with no money."

"Perfect targets for every lowlife wanting to take advantage of them,"

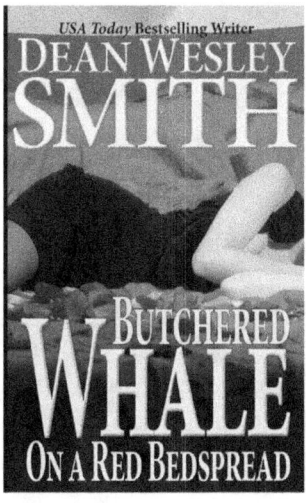

Sarge said, nodding and going back to putting on his shoes.

"Exactly," Pickett said. "We're running into professional ids right from year one with these girls, lots of money from the start, no mistakes at all that we can find, and a perfect way of killing targets."

Sarge looked at her. "Hard to imagine five sisters right out of the foster system having that kind of skill set just a year or so later."

"Bingo," Pickett said, feeling excited. "These sisters were trained and sponsored and if they were trained, who else was trained with them or since and who did the training?"

"Damn, you were right," Sarge said, looking suddenly worried, "this is a really horrid thought."

"We're dealing with professionals here, just as with the tunnel case," Pickett said.

She grabbed her cell phone out of her pocket. "I'll call Robin and Will, you warn Mike Dans to be careful with the marriage licenses."

Sarge moved quickly to the dresser and grabbed his cell phone as Pickett headed toward the kitchen with hers.

Their three kittens were all sleeping on the couch in the sun in the living room. Nose was on the back of the couch, Pete and Ree were stretched out on the cushions. Pickett knew those three kittens belonged together, just as she and Sarge did.

Robin answered and before she could say more than a word, Pickett told Robin what she and Sarge had come up with.

"Shit, shit, shit," Robin said when Pickett finished and hung up.

Pickett smiled at the phone and put it on the counter as Sarge came out of the bedroom.

"Mike hadn't gone in yet and will be cautious," Sarge said.

"Robin swore at me and hung up," Pickett said, laughing.

"I think you just kicked a hornet's nest here," Sarge said.

"Yeah, maybe so," Pickett said.

Sarge glanced over at the three sleeping kittens, then back at her. "You up for a nap before we head out.

Pickett smiled. "I would love that."

Sarge took her hand and they headed back into his bedroom to curl up together on his large bed.

Both of them had their cell phones with them. Even on a lazy Sunday afternoon, they were still detectives.

TWENTY-EIGHT

November 20th, 2016
Las Vegas, Nevada

THIRTY MINUTES LATER it was Pickett's cell phone that woke them up.

"Yeah," Pickett said.

Sarge stretched and tried to listen. He couldn't hear a thing.

Finally Picket said, "Hang on, I'm putting you on speakerphone. Tell us again what you just said."

She sat up on the edge of the bed and put her phone on the bed between them.

"Okay," Robin said as Pickett clicked on the speaker. "There is some pretty sophisticated tracking going on with each of the sister's last three names. Will and I are both pretty sure we didn't trigger anything and we have backed off completely now until we can work under the tracking."

"Tracking?" Pickett asked a half second before Sarge could.

"They are monitoring any kind of investigation into the sisters' driver's licenses, missing person reports, and so on. Anything under that name is being watched. Including the two open possible murder cases."

"Wow," Sarge said, sitting up on the bed and putting a few pillows behind his back against the headboard. He was now completely awake.

"You check into Strickland?" Pickett asked. "He's done an investigation on Buddy Charles' wife."

Robin laughed. "Henry isn't going to like this, but his systems were bugged. The downloads only happen from his system once a week and we managed to get in and block the next download."

"You want us to tell him," Sarge asked.

"Yeah," Pickett said, "but not in his office. It might be bugged as well. We can find no trace of any, but I would rather have him looking than us."

"These people are that sophisticated?" Pickett asked.

"They are and this approach has answered a lot of questions for Will," Robin said. "This is a well-funded operation which explains the money and the high level of fake backgrounds and ids."

Sarge just shook his head on that. How could this even be? And why? Why would anyone fund this sort of thing?

"We've expanded our search to other abusers who were killed," Robin said. "You would be amazed at how many cases of food poisoning are reported in Las Vegas every year."

"Not sure I want to know that," Sarge said, laughing.

"Considering how many millions of meals that are served in restaurants every day in this city," Robin said, "the chances are very, very slim of anyone having a problem."

"But it happens enough to cover up these murders," Pickett said.

"It does," Robin said. "And often these men who are targeted have other underlying health issues, mostly diabetes, bad hearts, or alcoholism, so often that is written down as a cause of death."

"Logical," Sarge said. He couldn't even begin to remember the numbers of dead body calls he got over the years. When a person was found dead, alone in a hotel room, it was always considered a crime scene until other causes were determined. And that meant a detective had to look at the scene. Many of the scenes and bodies had not been pretty.

"We're being very careful now with the searches," Robin said. "We're looking for the same pattern now with missing persons and men with records of abuse suddenly dying."

"We'll go talk with Strickland," Pickett said.

Robin laughed. "Have fun with that. Back with you when we have more."

Then she hung up.

Sarge looked at Pickett who had also moved to sit up on the edge of the big bed.

"What the hell have we stumbled into now?" Pickett asked, shaking her head.

"My guess would be a major vigilante operation," Sarge said. "More than likely, just as with the sisters, all for revenge."

Pickett nodded.

They sat there on the bed in silence, thinking.

Sarge knew that both of them had seen their fair share of women beaten by their husbands. And a few instances of men being beaten and killed by their wives. Nothing good ever came out of such crimes.

Sarge believed that the abusers should be punished and given help for their problems. And at times he had remembered walking into a scene that was so brutal he actually wanted to just pull out his gun and shoot the abuser.

But he never had and never would.

These women might be picking victims that were, on the surface, bad people. But it did not excuse serial murder.

Nothing did.

TWENTY-NINE

November 20th, 2016
Las Vegas, Nevada

HENRY STRICKLAND WAS stunned that they called him on a Sunday afternoon, but he agreed to meet them outside his office in thirty minutes.

Pickett splashed some water on her face and then got a bottle of water for her and for Sarge out of his fridge. The three kittens had moved from the couch to spots along the window, still in the sun. Like most cats, they didn't notice that she and Sarge left.

The Sunday afternoon traffic was light and the day had never really gotten warm, although the sky was a deep, rich blue.

The drive was easy and when they got to Strickland's office, Sarge got out and moved to the back seat as Strickland came out and climbed in the front.

"So I'm assuming there is a reason for meeting in the car and not in there," Strickland said as he closed the door.

"We're afraid your office might be bugged," Sarge said.

Strickland actually laughed at that. "Not a chance in hell."

That was exactly the reaction Pickett expected him to have.

"Your computer system was bugged," Pickett said. "Robin and Will found it and got it stopped from its weekly download of your files."

Strickland opened his mouth and then closed it again. Then he asked, clearly anger in his voice, "Why and how did you know to even look?"

Pickett held up her hand for him to stop.

"Robin will send you the information about the bug," Pickett said. "Beyond my level. The reason is because of your case investigating Buddy Charles' wife."

"The five sisters are that sophisticated?" Strickland asked.

"No," Sarge said. "We don't think so. We think there is an organization, a sponsor of some sort that has trained them and been behind them for the last seventeen years."

"Oh, shit," Strickland said.

"That's why the incredible new identities," Pickett said, "and where all the money it would cost a sister to set up a new life every year came from."

"Got any idea who?" Strickland asked, shaking his head.

"Nothing yet," Sarge said. "These people are good, really good. We may never find them."

"But we are worried that they may be backing more vigilantes than just the sisters," Pickett said.

"So check your office," Sarge said. "Carefully. These people are damned good, as we said. Maybe have Mike come in and help you with the check to be sure. He's got all the best equipment to make sure everything is clear."

Strickland nodded. "I'll call Mike at once. From out here."

Pickett liked the private detective. He was rolling with this and doing what needed to be done.

"So what can I do to help?" Strickland asked.

"First off," Pickett said, "you call Mike and get him on the way, then call Robin and she and Will can explain the bug in your computer system and how it worked."

Strickland nodded.

"Then after you feel you are completely clean," Pickett said, "we could use your help searching your files for other cases that could be vigilante. Bad people getting what seemed to be coming to them. Or missing person cases that seem to make sense if looked at from this angle."

"You'll need to do it alone," Sarge said. "On a closed system. Have Mike help you set that up."

"I will," Strickland said. "Thank you for this. I owe you both one. I'll call if I find even a whiff of strangeness. I want to catch these bastards just for the chance of punching one of them in the face for hacking my system."

Pickett and Sarge both laughed as Strickland got out and moved over to the sidewalk in front of his office to call Mike.

Sarge got out and climbed into the front seat, then said simply, in his cold, calm voice, "Pull away from here, get out of sight and stop and park."

Pickett looked at him, feeling stunned, but did as he said as Sarge pulled out his phone.

"Robin," Sarge said. "Are you guys good enough to find out who Strickland is talking to right now on his cell phone? Or who he just called in the last minute or so?"

Sarge nodded. "Just a gut sense is all. And check that bug that was in his system. How long had it been there?"

Sarge nodded as Pickett pulled the car over in front of an empty lot and parked it.

"I hope I am wrong about this," Sarge said as he clicked his phone onto speaker.

Some Classic Dean Wesley Smith Stories
Available at your favorite booksellers.

"Shit, shit, shit!!" Robin said a few second later. "That bug was in his system for over ten years."

"Afraid of that," Sarge said. "It wasn't a bug, just an easy way to report in."

And Will's voice came in from the back. "You are never going to believe who Strickland just called. James Newell."

Pickett felt her stomach clamp up and Sarge's eyes were round.

"You're sure?" Pickett asked softly.

"Completely sure," Will's voice said from the background.

"He's calling Mike now," Robin said.

"We told him to," Pickett said. "So he's going to have to do that."

"After he is done with the call to Mike, let me know," Sarge said. "I'll call Mike, tell him what is happening."

"And we'll dig for a history of abuse in James' family," Robin said.

"Check his computer files that you got from the bug," Sarge said. "I'm betting buried in that there are files on all five sisters and maybe others doing similar things."

"Will do," Robin said. "I'll call you when Strickland is off the phone with Mike." Then she hung up.

Sarge pocketed his phone.

Pickett just sat there, feeling stunned. Finally she turned to Sarge.

"What tipped you to Strickland?"

"Coincidence at first," Sarge said. "He's had his firm for exactly seventeen years."

Pickett nodded. "I saw that as well."

"His tone when you told him there was a bug in his system," Sarge said. "He wasn't angry about the bug being there, he was angry at Will and Robin for getting into his system and finding it. He covered quickly, but that shocked him."

Pickett nodded. "I thought his reaction was as I expected. I only heard the anger, not what it was directed at. Great spot."

"Also," Sarge said, "when we told him about the five sisters, he was stunned we knew that, not surprised at the information."

"Missed all of that," Pickett said, shaking her head. "And it's obvious now that you point it out."

"That's why the three of us are partners," Sarge said. "We all see different things. But sure sorry to have James involved with this."

"There would have to be a reason," Pickett said. "So not going to believe it until we find that reason."

Sarge nodded and said nothing.

She sure hoped in her heart that Strickland calling James would turn out to be something else. Anything else.

But her detective gut told her it wouldn't.

PART SIX
The Big Play

THIRTY

November 20th, 2016
Las Vegas, Nevada

PICKETT DECIDED TO move them away from Strickland's office so Sarge suggested they head to the Bellagio for Sunday dinner.

Robin called Sarge back as Pickett got them headed down the Strip. "Strickland is off the phone with Mike."

Sarge said, "Thanks."

This was going to be tough to explain to Mike, but he had to do it and do it quickly.

Mike picked up on the first ring. "Sarge, what can I do for you?"

"When are you meeting Strickland?"

"Tomorrow morning in his office," Mike said. "He wants me to check for bugs and set up an area of his office with a secure work station."

"Yeah," Sarge said, "we told him to call you and ask for just that. But there is a major problem. We are pretty sure Strickland is one of the people behind a long string of murders."

"Oh, great," Mike said.

Sarge could almost see Mike just shaking his head.

"I owe you dinner," Sarge said. "You got time for dinner and a long, complicated story involving five sisters?"

"Bellagio?" Mike asked.

"We're already headed there," Sarge said.

"See you in fifteen," Mike said and hung up.

Sarge nodded to Pickett. "He's on his way."

At that moment Pickett's phone rang and she handed it to Sarge.

He put it on speaker and said, "We're here and on our way to meet Mike for dinner."

"Bellagio?" Robin asked.

"Where else?" Pickett said, laughing.

"Wish I could join you, but I think I need to stay right here at my computer," Robin said. "The reason I called is that we found some ugly history in James' family."

"Oh, no," Pickett said softly.

Robin went on. "James' father abused his mother and his sister. His sister killed herself when she was thirteen. A year later his father was caught raping a twelve-year-old girl and arrested. He was killed in jail by another inmate."

"Oh, no," Pickett said.

Sarge felt sick to his stomach. He knew how much both Pickett and Robin liked James. This was going to be difficult at best for both of them. Right now Pickett was focusing on the road and traffic around her, but her jaw was set and her face pale.

"James' mother died while he was away in college," Robin said. "Causes unknown."

Only the traffic noise cut through the silence in the car. Sarge just felt sick to his stomach. He couldn't imagine how Pickett was feeling.

"We're looking into Strickland's family history," Robin said. "Just thought you would want to know about James."

With that she hung up.

Sarge looked at Pickett who was just shaking her head as she drove.

After a moment she said softly, "How could Robin and I have not seen this?"

"He helped you with cases, didn't he?" Sarge asked.

Pickett nodded.

"I bet his wife doesn't even know, and as far as James is concerned, he's just protecting the innocent like no one protected his sister."

"He thinks he's actually helping people?"

"He does," Sarge said. "But my worry is back to how are we going to prove any of this? We have lots and lots of circumstantial evidence that would get this case tossed out of court in a heartbeat. Especially if we accused someone with the reputation and money that James has."

"And we still don't know where the five sisters are," Pickett said as she pulled into the Bellagio parking lot.

"And if there are more killers besides the five sisters out there setting up their targets right now," Sarge said.

Actually, that was what worried him the most. Every day this took them to solve, the more chance someone was going to die.

THIRTY-ONE

November 20th, 2016
Las Vegas, Nevada

PICKETT WANTED TO just hit something. She and Robin had trusted James, maybe more than they should have at times. But he had been a good friend, a generous donor to charities, and seemingly a good citizen of Las Vegas.

Now they were thinking about him for the money and brains behind a serial killing spree. This couldn't be right. But having Strickland call him right after they had that conversation was very damning.

And his background didn't help the reasonable doubt either. But as Sarge said, they had no real case. They had a lot of suspicions and connections, but no evidence.

So she needed to believe in James for the moment and not completely hang him without evidence.

And as careful as Strickland and the five sisters were, and maybe James as well, they might never find actual evidence.

Pickett and Sarge walked in silence on a sidewalk beside the parking lot and into the Bellagio Casino. The late afternoon air had a chill to it and inside the door of the casino the sounds of people laughing and talking and bells ringing grounded Pickett a little more.

She took Sarge's hand as they headed along the wide tile walkway toward the café.

As they got to the entrance of the café, she looked up at Sarge. "Really glad you are here with me on this one."

He smiled and squeezed her hand. "I'm glad to be anywhere with you."

She laughed. "Wow, a fast and perfect answer."

She kissed him.

He just laughed and said, "The truth is always a good answer."

"In this case, yes," Pickett said, laughing.

And laughing made her feel better. Still angry, but at least thinking again.

Amazingly, their regular booth was open back among the plants and they gave the woman who seated them their drink order of two coffees and glasses of water.

The booth had a large oak-colored table and leather seats and plants ringed the back of it giving it a sense of privacy. The noise was louder in the restaurant than normal, mostly because it was the dinner rush. And there were a lot of tourists walking by along the front of the café pulling suitcases.

Mike seemed to appear out of nowhere as they were getting settled.

He was a solid man, all muscle, with wide shoulders and close-cropped hair. He was former Special Forces but never talked about his background. He had intense eyes that never seemed to miss a detail, yet a smile that could relax anyone around him. He was also one of the smartest people Pickett had ever met, and that was going some.

Pickett had liked him from the moment she had met him a month earlier. Robin and Will thought he was the best there was in the business at security and finding things. And the team of former

Special Forces men he had working for him were amazing.

Mike gave the waitress his drink order when she brought the water and coffee and they all ordered dinner at that point as well, since they all knew the menu so well.

Mike had a rare top sirloin with a baker, Sarge had a chef's salad, which was huge, and Pickett decided she wanted halibut with a dinner salad.

Mike then took out his notebook and pen and asked, "What the hell is going on?"

Starting from the beginning, they told Mike about the case, the five sisters, their discussion with the husbands, the poisoning of the abusive men in the hotels, and so on.

When he got to how many men they thought had been killed, he just shook his head and kept writing.

Then Sarge told him about the conversation with Strickland, his reactions, and how Will and Robin had traced the fact that he had called James Newell the moment they had left, before calling Mike.

"The James Newell?" Mike asked, clearly shocked. "The architect, the same one you went to for help with the older hotels?"

Pickett nodded. She then filled Mike in on what Robin had found about James' background.

Mike sat back, thinking as the dinners arrived. They all started to eat in silence until Mike said, "So you think Newell is the money behind all this and Strickland the general in the field?"

"Pretty much," Sarge said. "And we don't have a damn bit of evidence on any of it that we can prove. So we could be completely wrong."

"I'm still hoping we're wrong about James Newell being involved in some way," Pickett said. "But my gut tells me we aren't."

"A friend?" Mike asked.

Pickett nodded. That was all she felt safe doing at that moment. She focused on her halibut, knowing it tasted good, but not being able to really enjoy it.

"So at the moment only the three of us and Robin and Will have this entire picture?" Mike asked.

Pickett and Sarge both nodded.

The three of them ate in silence until finally Mike said, "How do you two get into this kind of stuff?"

Sarge laughed lightly. "We've been asking ourselves that same question."

"But the problem is that we can't really prove what we have found," Pickett said. "We can't confirm any of it."

"And for all we know," Sarge said, "there are more killers out there besides the five sisters."

That thought made Pickett push away the rest of her dinner.

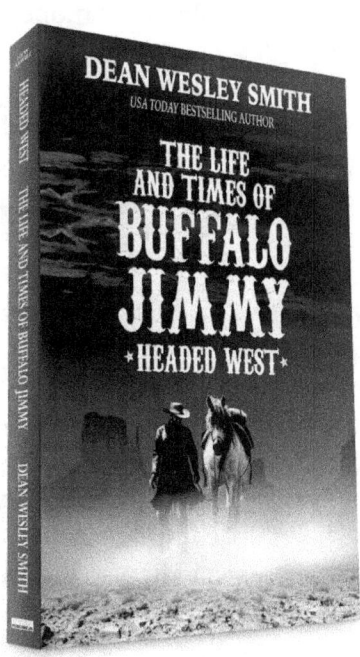

"We need to prove this, Mike," Sarge said. "Somehow."

Mike nodded.

"And if we can't prove it enough to put anyone in jail," Pickett said. "We have to at least stop it."

Sarge and Mike nodded.

And Pickett knew that they both wouldn't feel satisfied with that result.

She wouldn't either.

THIRTY-TWO

November 20th, 2016
Las Vegas, Nevada

THEY FINISHED THEIR meals and were drinking coffee, still helping Mike fill in what gaps they could, when Sarge came back to the question he had been asking all along.

"We need to follow the money," Sarge said.

He knew that was one of the major keys on this. And now, if the money led back to Newell, as they suspected it did, that would help.

Mike sat forward. "What are you thinking?"

"These five sisters must start lives over every year," Sarge said. "That has to be expensive."

"Just new wardrobes of clothes that don't look all new would take time and money to put together," Pickett said. "And they all buy at some point under the new name a car and rent an apartment and furnish it. Not cheap."

"We have the women's names and details for seventeen years," Sarge said.

"There has to be a money trail to each of them from somewhere."

"And the marriage license information you wanted me to get is to see if a couple of the women are applying for new marriage licenses?" Mike asked.

"If we can just spot one of them," Sarge said, "we might have it easier to track."

"But you said these women are setting up the next target family before they leave the one they are with. Right?" Mike asked.

"So right now all five of them are spending money for yet a new life," Pickett said.

"You think any of this information is going to be on Strickland's computer?" Mike asked.

"I don't think so," Sarge said. "Even with the bug reporting device on there, I can't imagine Strickland being that careless."

"Neither can I," Pickett said. "And if Newell is involved in this, I know he never would let anything get to him either."

Sarge sat back. He couldn't believe what he was thinking, but it was the only answer that made sense on all of this.

"They have a headquarters," Sarge said.

Pickett looked at him, frowning.

Mike slowly nodded.

"More than likely a store front," Sarge said, "a perfectly normal legit business of some sort, that everything concerning the sisters and maybe other killers, goes through."

"A charity," Pickett said.

Sarge knew she was right. He was about to suggest that she call Robin, but Pickett already had her phone to her ear.

"Makes sense," Mike said, nodding. "And that would give Strickland and Newell and who knows who else cover."

"Robin," Pickett said after a moment, "Sarge thinks there might be a headquarters for all this, some legit business or charity to give Newell and Strickland and others cover."

Pickett nodded. Then she clicked off her phone and set it on the table next to her coffee.

"Robin and Will and their people," Pickett said, "of which they have five working right now, are going to see if there are any patterns in the five sisters' shopping habits and credit card purchases."

"So back to the murders for a moment," Mike said. "You think one of the women lures an abuser into the hotel and the other is waiting there with Croton Oil to poison the guy. Right?"

"Croton Oil is tough to detect if not looked for," Pickett said. "And it mimics food poisoning right up to the point the victim falls into a coma and dies."

"Takes about fifteen minutes to work," Sarge said, "which would give the women time to escape, yet that is a short enough time that the victim would never be able to figure out what happened and talk."

"Every victim we have traced," Pickett said, "has died alone in a hotel room or from food poisoning or something related to a health condition that could have been triggered by Croton Oil."

Sarge had a hunch Mike was going somewhere with this line of questioning, so he just waited.

Mike nodded to all this, then asked, "So the theory is that these women marry these men to get into the family and do research?"

"That's the theory," Sarge said. "They are very careful and each victim we have looked closely at has been an abuser, of that there is no doubt."

Mike nodded. "So my guess is that in those retreats the sisters take, they are researching families of men they have met. If no abuser in the family, they don't bother to get to know the man better."

Sarge nodded. "And doing it from a remote location in a hotel room would make sure that nothing about the search could be traced later."

"Exactly," Mike said.

At that moment Pickett's cell rang.

She picked it up and said, "You want this on speaker?"

Sarge watched as Pickett glanced around. "Booth area is clear. I'll warn you if someone is approaching."

With that Pickett put the phone on speaker and set the phone in the middle of the table between them.

"Women's thrift store," Robin said, "out near the old Boulder Highway. Sells used clothing and furniture and donates to a number of women's shelters around the city."

Sarge nodded. That would make sense and explain part of how the sisters got new/used clothes every time they had to restart a life.

"The store has existed for seventeen years," Robin said.

"Could have guessed that," Pickett said. Mike nodded.

"Every incarnation of the five sisters that we have traced so far has spent money in that store," Robin said.

"Still no proof," Sarge said.

"James Newell is a major donor to the store," Robin said. "Right from the beginning."

"Damn it," Pickett said, softly.

"And Strickland does regular work for them," Robin said. "Also right from the beginning."

"Okay," Sarge said, leaning back and looking around to make sure no one was listening. "Lots of coincidences there."

"Mike," Robin said, "Will and I can only dig so far."

"I'll get myself and a few others on it tonight," Mike said.

"Thank you," Robin said. "We found a few alarms along the way, but nothing you won't be able to get past if you need to. For a small thrift store, they have a very sophisticated computer system."

Sarge sat forward on that. "More sophisticated than would be needed to run just five sisters in what we have learned?"

"Far more," Robin said.

"Shit," Mike said.

Sarge could only agree with that.

THIRTY-THREE

November 20th, 2016
Las Vegas, Nevada

PICKETT FELT LIKE they were making progress and with Robin and Will and all their computer people on the trail, and tonight Mike and his people would dig even deeper, they might be able to actually get to the bottom of all this.

But she was honestly worried about where the bottom of this cesspool of murder actually was. And how many people were swimming in it.

The sun had long set by the time they left the Bellagio. The air had a sharp bite to it and a slight wind from the north made it feel even colder.

After Pickett got her car started and actually turned on the heat, she suggested to Sarge that they take a drive out along the old Boulder Highway, not to stop at the thrift store, but to just take a look at it.

Sarge agreed. Both of them wanted a look at what they might be facing. More than likely they would never have to

even go in the place, but it still felt right to go look.

She got onto Flamingo and headed east until she ran into the Boulder Highway and then turned right.

The old Boulder Highway had, at one time, been the main road out of Las Vegas, heading up to the town of Boulder. But a faster freeway had left the old highway with scattered nineteen-fifties' hotels, warehouses, and empty lots where businesses used to exist.

The thrift store occupied what had been a small market at one point and looked to be pretty good sized. It sat on a large lot with a cracked and old parking lot completely around it. Two of the dozen parking lot lights still worked, but only barely.

Pickett didn't slow as she drove past, then went four more blocks and turned around in an old Burger King parking lot and headed back.

As they passed the thrift store the second time, Sarge said simply, "I'm betting there's something under that parking lot."

Pickett could see what he meant. The land was far, far bigger and the parking lot far larger than was needed for even an old market, let alone a thrift store. There had been no reason to ever pave it all.

He took out his phone and called Robin, putting it on speaker as Pickett headed them back into downtown and toward the Ogden which she could see towering next to the casinos ahead.

"Robin," Sarge said. "We just did a drive-by of the thrift store. Any old plans or permits for a large basement under that store and the parking lot around it?"

"Didn't see any," Robin said. "But didn't look that closely at the history yet."

"Also check the power bill for that place," Pickett said, realizing what she had seen without noticing it. The power line running to that building was much larger than needed.

Sarge nodded.

"We'll check on both and call you back," Robin said.

"What do you think might be under there?" Pickett asked. "If anything?"

"With this case," Sarge said, "I would be afraid to even take a guess."

Pickett laughed at that. "I'm hoping for evidence."

"Yeah," Sarge said. "We can only hope. But not holding my breath. These people have been far too smart for far too long."

"And dangerous as well," Pickett said.

Sarge only nodded at that.

Once she parked in her spot in the underground parking garage of the Ogden and they were walking toward the elevator, she asked, "Up for a movie?"

"I would love one," he said, smiling at her. "Try to take my mind off of this case."

"I might be able to help with that after the movie as well," Pickett said, smiling at the man she was in love with.

"If we're still awake by then," he said.

"Oh, wow," she said, pretending to frown as they got into the elevator. "You sure know how to give a girl a complex."

He laughed and kissed her as they rode up the elevator to the penthouse level.

They had almost made it to his bedroom with Sarge doing his best to make sure she didn't have a complex, as she said, when Robin called them back.

"Complex interruptus," he said, laughing as she took out her phone and they moved into the kitchen.

"On speaker," Pickett said, putting the phone on the counter. "We're in Sarge's kitchen."

"Good spot on the basement of the thrift store," Robin said. "It's the size of

a large warehouse down there. And the entire place pulls a lot of power at times."

"Printers and computer levels of power?" Pickett asked.

"Even more at times," Robin said. "Will thinks that's where they make the fake ids, but that wouldn't take that kind of power or space. Something else is going on in that basement."

"Maybe Mike will find out what?" Sarge said.

"We hope so," Robin said. "Will and I have dug about as far as we dare dig without warrants and we have not one shred of evidence to even try to get a warrant."

Pickett nodded.

"We understand that," Sarge said.

"Make sure your alarms are on tonight," Robin said. "We kicked a hornet's nest today and we have no idea how they might respond."

"Copy that," Pickett said. "You two have a good night. See you at breakfast?"

"I'll be there," Robin said.

"Breakfast is here tomorrow morning," Sarge said. "These people use poison as a normal way of killing. We take no chances."

Pickett stared at Sarge for a moment, then nodded.

"See you for breakfast at your place then," Robin said after a moment. "Gives me a chance to see the kittens again."

With that she hung up.

"Well that was a mood killer," Pickett said, shaking her head as she clicked off her phone.

"I'll make the popcorn," Sarge said.

"I'll go get changed," Pickett said.

"And I'll feed the kittens their snack. You know that Nose has already moved in."

Sarge pointed to the couch where Nose, Pete, and Ree all were sound asleep on the couch together.

Pickett laughed. "She's just a little ahead of me is all."

"Not by much, I hope."

Pickett kissed Sarge. "Not by much, I promise."

She headed for the door to go to her place to get changed. She loved the idea Sarge had of knocking an archway between the two condos. Maybe, as soon as they got this case finished, they would do that.

All they had to do was find some evidence.

Maybe she would move in before the case wrapped up, since real evidence was something they were in very short supply of at the moment.

Very short, as in none at all.

THIRTY-FOUR

November 21st, 2016
Las Vegas, Nevada

SARGE WAS ENJOYING cooking breakfast for Pickett and Robin. Both of them had offered to help, but he had told them they could help by keeping the kittens entertained and refilling his coffee when it got low.

He managed to actually get them some ham and cheese omelets that looked pretty good, a small slice of ham, and toast and get it all out almost at the same time.

They all went to the table upstairs that showed the late-fall morning out over Las Vegas. It looked a little cold and gray and cloudy, but the view made up for anything like that.

"I keep forgetting how spectacular the view is from up here," Robin said as she put out a pitcher of orange juice and a coffee pot.

Sarge had just put all three of their plates on the table and Pickett was bringing up the coffee cups and a pot of coffee for refills.

"It really is stunning," Pickett said.

"I can't imagine ever getting used to it," Sarge said. And he couldn't. It seemed fresh every time he came up to this level.

Earlier in the month he and Pickett came up here on warm evenings and just sat with a glass of wine on the balcony and talked and stared at the view of the city. He was already looking forward to the spring when the weather would allow them for a time to do that again.

"So Will's people didn't find much more last night," Robin said after they all settled in to eat. "On the surface that thrift shop does some fantastic charity work for women's issues around town."

"On the surface?" Pickett asked right before Sarge could.

"Nothing we can find other than that," Robin said. "And no reason at all for that basement."

They talked while they ate and at one point had a great laugh at all three kittens chasing each other up the stairs, around them, and then back down. Sarge could not tell which kitten was doing the chasing. They seemed to take turns all in mid-stride.

They had just started into their coffee when Sarge's phone rang. He knew from the number it was Mike.

"Any luck?" Sarge asked as he clicked on the phone.

"More than expected," Mike said. "You guys at the Nugget?"

"My place," Sarge said. "All three of us."

"I'm ten minutes out," Mike said. "I need to tell you three some of this in person."

He hung up and Sarge put the phone back in his shirt pocket and looked at the concerned faces of Pickett and Robin. "Mike's on his way with news."

Both nodded and all three of them stood and gathered up the dishes and headed down to the kitchen. They had breakfast cleaned up and the dishwasher going as Mike rang the bell.

Sarge poured him a cup of coffee and they all four went back upstairs to talk.

"Wow," Mike said, looking around at the view. "This can't be beat."

"That I agree," Sarge said.

"So here's the news," Mike said. "That basement is a sanctuary for abused women."

Sarge sat back. That was not at all what he was expecting.

"In fact," Mike said, "It's one of three in the city for women and there is one for men as well, completely hidden, and part of a nationwide underground-railroad type of operation."

Robin looked at Mike. "So they get women and kids new ids, money, a new place to live, and get them out of town and away from abusive husbands?"

"Exactly," Mike said. "Each sanctuary has family living centers, counselors, and a hospital area for injuries."

Sarge kept shaking his head. He knew there were women's shelters around town, but in all his years as a cop he had never heard of anything like this.

Pickett seemed as stunned as he felt.

"Women from other cities are coming into Las Vegas," Mike said, "with new lives and abused women from here are sent to other places."

"This sounds amazing," Robin said.

"So if these five sisters have this sort of resource," Pickett said, "why are they killing abusive men instead of just rescuing the women and kids?"

"Some women don't want to be rescued," Sarge said, softly, remembering more than he wanted to remember of beat-up women who refused to press charges against their husbands.

All three of the others nodded. They had all seen it far, far too often. And far, far too often the women and sometimes the children ended up dead in short order.

They all sat silent for a moment, then Mike said, "There is no doubt that both Strickland and Newell are connected to this women's shelter. Both are part of a fairly large donor network and Strickland does work for the shelter when needed. More than likely helping them set up safe homes for the women and families coming in here in Las Vegas."

"So we have a network of underground shelters doing great work," Robin said, "and five serial killer sisters that might or might not be linked to the shelter in some way."

Pickett nodded.

Mike just sort of looked pained.

"And if they are linked to the shelter or the deaths," Sarge said, "we still are sitting here without a lick of evidence to prove any of it."

"I feel almost dirty now even trying," Pickett said.

Sarge could only nod to that. He had no idea what they should do next except keep on trying to find the killers, if the women were the killers, and hope they weren't connected to the shelters in any way.

He had a hunch they were connected, but not in any way that could be proven.

And he was convinced that all the good people working at the shelter would know nothing about the five sisters killing abusive men.

This case had just become a no-win case.

And he hated that.

PART SEVEN
Freezeout…The End Game

THIRTY-FIVE

November 21st, 2016
Las Vegas, Nevada

PICKETT HATED WITH a passion how this case had turned. Over the years as a detective, she had always liked cases that were more black and white, good versus bad, cops versus murderers.

This case was so far from black and white, she didn't know what to do. Even though she couldn't prove it in any way, she knew she had five sisters who had killed at least eighty-five men.

The fact that the men were abusive husbands didn't matter. They were human beings and the sisters had choices other than cold-blooded murder.

But now there was a chance the sisters were tied into a person she considered a good friend, James Newell, and also a women's shelter that clearly did the work of saints in helping protect women and families.

But they had no proof on that either.

All speculations.

And not even Mike, with all his computer specialty work, could make any link at all with Newell, Strickland, the five sisters, or the women's shelter under the thrift store.

"So we're at a dead end," Sarge said.

The four of them were still sitting at the table in his loft, the fantastic view of the city around them.

Robin and Mike nodded.

"I hate this," Pickett said. "There has to be some way we can tie those sisters to at least one murder without dragging down the shelter at the same time."

"That's what we work on then," Robin said.

Sarge nodded. "And we have to find the sisters and stop them before they kill again, remember."

Pickett agreed to that. It seemed at this point that was all they could do.

Mike left to get back to work and Pickett and Sarge and Robin sat staring into space, trying to figure out what to do next.

Pickett had not one idea.

Not one.

"Facial recognition," Sarge said. "Possible to develop a program that would scan for faces from grocery stores, drug stores, traffic cams, places like that?"

Robin nodded. "Long shot and a lot of data. But we might get lucky and find one of them."

"And if we find a sister," Pickett asked, "then what?"

As she expected, neither Sarge nor Robin had an answer to that one. But she knew they had to try.

"So what else can we do on this fine Monday?" Pickett asked.

"I have to go shopping," Sarge said, smiling. "I was hoping I could cook a turkey dinner on Thursday for you two and Will and maybe a few others from the Cold Poker Gang who didn't have anywhere to go."

Pickett looked stunned. "Didn't know you could cook a turkey dinner."

"Used to all the time," he said. "But the last few years just went out. But this year, if you two would like, I can give it another try."

Pickett smiled and kissed him. "I would love that."

And she would. It sounded wonderful.

"Count me and Will in as well," Robin said.

At that moment Robin's phone rang. She glanced at the phone and Pickett watched Robin's face go white.

"It's James," Robin said.

"Well," Sarge said, "we did kick his nest a little yesterday."

Pickett felt as surprised as Robin looked.

Robin clicked on the phone and said, "Hi, James. Can I put you on speaker? Pickett and Sarge are here as well."

She nodded and clicked on the speaker and put the phone down on the table between them.

"Hi, James," Pickett said.

"Robin, Pickett, Sarge, great talking with you again," James said.

Pickett was surprised that his voice sounded perfectly normal and not in the slightest bit stressed.

"What can we do for you, James?" Robin asked.

"Actually," James said, "It's what I can do for you. I know you three have been looking into a special thrift store out on the Boulder Highway. Thought you might want a tour."

"We would love one," Robin said. "Very kind of you."

Robin's eyes were round and Pickett was as surprised as Robin was looking.

Sarge just sat there shaking his head.

"I can be there in about one hour," James said, "if you three are free."

"We are," Robin said.

"See you then," James said.

Robin clicked off the phone and then just stared at it.

"What just happened there?"

"He seems to know everything we are doing," Sarge said.

Sarge picked up the phone and hit a call number. After a moment Sarge said, "Mike, need your help in two areas."

Sarge nodded.

"We just got a call from Newell offering to show us the shelter in one hour."

"Back-up would be fantastic, thanks," Sarge said after a moment. "And could you sweep my condo and Pickett's condo for bugs? Newell seems to know what we are doing at any moment."

Sarge nodded. "Thanks."

Sarge hung up. "Mike and his people will have us covered completely if something happens in that shelter. He's going to meet us in thirty-five minutes at the Burger King down the road from the shelter and give us bugs and tracking pins that should work through any kind of blocks. Plus he'll track our phones."

Pickett nodded. "Really good thinking."

"I just wish I knew what the hell we were walking into," Robin said.

"Just don't touch or eat or drink anything," Sarge said, smiling.

"Not funny," Pickett said.

"Yeah," Robin said.

Sarge just chuckled.

Ten minutes later Pickett was pulling out of the underground garage and turning to head out the Boulder Highway. She had a hunch that one way or another, they were going to get some answers on all this very soon.

She just had no idea what the answers might be.

THIRTY-SIX

November 21st, 2016
Las Vegas, Nevada

SARGE MADE SURE his tracking button was secure and well-hidden. And that his gun was loaded. He had no idea what they were walking into here, but considering they had no other real leads, this seemed to be the only solution.

Just under one hour from when they had said they would meet Newell, Pickett pulled her SUV into the driveway of the thrift store and parked in the parking area around back.

The lot was larger than it had looked from the street and if all of that was open underground, it would be huge. And there wasn't the slightest bit of evidence that anything existed under the old, cracked pavement.

The morning air still had a bite to it, but the day promised to be a nice one. As they were headed toward the front of the thrift shop, James Newell drove in.

He parked his white Cadillac four-door next to Pickett's SUV and the three of them waited for him to get out and join them.

"Thanks for the tour," Robin said as he approached.

"I was expecting to give it the moment you two came out to my house," Newell said. He pointed around at the vast parking lot. "We're all pretty proud of the work we do here. And in other three sanctuaries like it around the city."

Sarge just nodded and neither Pickett nor Robin said a word.

Newell led them through the front door of the thrift shop and said "hi" to a woman working behind the counter. Sarge missed her name, but Newell pointed to the three of them.

"Three of Las Vegas' finest detectives."

The woman nodded, looked around to make sure no one else was in the shop and pushed a button.

A shelf with lots of junk kitchen items on the back wall swung open and Newell led the way in behind it.

A bright light came up behind the shelf and showed a clean and modern staircase heading down.

Pickett glanced at Sarge, clearly not happy that in less than a month two cases had taken them underground. Sarge had to admit he wasn't that happy about it either.

At the bottom of the stairs was a large metal door.

Newel punched in a code he didn't let them see into a lock box and the door swung open.

Beyond was a reception area that looked like a modern hospital reception area. It was bright, with modern furniture,

and a smiling woman sitting behind the desk. A large screen television showed changing desert shots on one wall, giving the sense the room had windows.

The woman was thin, in her middle thirties, maybe, and looked completely in shape. She had on a white blouse and dress slacks.

"Hi, James," the woman said, standing and coming around from behind the desk. "Thanks for giving us some warning on guests coming through. We have a couple new admissions that we needed to clear from the public areas to help them feel safe."

"Completely understand," James said. "Thanks for allowing this tour. These are three detective friends of mine from the Las Vegas force. They can be trusted without fail."

Sarge felt shocked at what James had just said and clearly Pickett and Robin felt the same way. The three of them had just spent a lot of time possibly endangering this entire enterprise. So clearly James was betting that when they saw the place, it might make them forget about eighty-five murders.

Sarge just shook his head. Not likely and James clearly wasn't a stupid man. He knew Pickett and Robin would never do that, so there had to be another reason for this tour.

Beyond the door behind the receptionist area, there was a large living area. All modern, all decorated with plants. Five or six seating areas with modern couches, chairs, and coffee tables filled the space. Everything was done in light tan, wood, and brown tones and to Sarge the place felt comfortable, and again gave no sense of being underground at all.

That was helped by the varying ceiling height through the place. One area would have tall ceilings, another area the ceilings were down lower for a more intimate feel.

Clearly James had done some designing on this and it had worked.

Across the way was what looked to be a community kitchen with three or four different-sized dining tables.

And past that was a large playground, with slides and all the modern stuff for kids to play on.

There was no one to be seen.

Sarge glanced around. The receptionist had not come with them, but the door still stood slightly ajar behind them.

"Wow," Robin said.

"This is stunning and very comfortable," Pickett said.

Sarge had to agree with both of them.

The hallways leading off in three directions," James said, pointing at the three, "are to family apartments. Each apartment has a full living room, kitchen, dining area, and bedrooms. All fully furnished. Groceries are delivered every day for what each woman or family needs and asks for."

"All secured?" Sarge asked.

"Completely," James said. "But we have never had an issue here because we are so careful in extracting the women from their situations. And everything is blocked completely down here, including the audio Mike Dans helped you into a little bit ago. However, we left your trackers on so Mike and his people wouldn't worry."

"Is Mike working for you?" Sarge asked.

James laughed. "Oh, heavens, no. But I respect him and admire him and his team and what he does."

"Sounds like you have a pretty good team of your own," Robin said.

"We do," James said, nodding. "It's required to keep these women safe and get them the professional counseling help they need to get restarted in life. Plus get them moved and into a new life."

Now Sarge had to admit he was impressed. But he figured it was time to lay all their cards on the table since it was clear James and his people had been far, far ahead of them all along.

"So what about the five Jones sisters?" Sarge asked.

"They vanished, it seems, within an hour of the two of you showing up at my house," James said, smiling at Sarge and Pickett. "I had no doubt that the three of you would eventually find them. Eventually."

"And where are they now?" Pickett asked.

James just shook his head. "I honestly have no idea. I wish I did."

Sarge just stared at James for a moment. Pickett looked shocked.

James indicated they move to a table. "Let's sit down so I can tell you the entire story as I know it."

Sarge wasn't so sure he wanted to sit with this man, but he would at least give James some rope to hang himself.

THIRTY-SEVEN

November 21st, 2016
Las Vegas, Nevada

PICKETT WASN'T SURE what she was the most stunned about. The fantastic and modern facility hidden under an old parking lot or the fact that a man she had trusted had just admitted knowing about five serial killers.

They all sat down at the table and Pickett sat back. She wasn't at all sure she wanted to hear this story. But she was willing to listen, to see if they could find any path to real evidence.

"First off," James said, "I want to tell you how pleased I am that you three managed to take this as far as you have."

"Sounds sort of condescending," Robin said.

Pickett felt the same way.

"It was not intended that way," James said, looking worried. "When I called Andor and suggested he give the three of you this case, this was exactly what I was hoping for. Exactly."

"You called Andor?" Sarge said a half second before Pickett could.

James nodded. "I only learned about the five sisters about two months ago and I was appalled to say the least. Shocked and disgusted and yet I had no evidence at all to go to anyone about what was happening."

Sarge waved his hands in the air and said, "Let's just stop right there. Would you start over from the beginning, back when you built and designed this place, and what it is all connected to?"

"And then work us to the sisters," Robin said.

James nodded and took a deep breath. "I am certain you have researched my family history and the abusive father I had."

Pickett nodded, as did the other two.

"When I started to attain a level of money, I started to look around for areas where I could help others and I came across these shelters. That was over twenty years ago and the shelters at that time were mostly just houses where women tried to protect abused women from their abusers."

Pickett knew all that. As a detective, she had been to her fair share of those homes on emergency calls as an abused wife tried to hide from an angry and usually drunk husband. In one case the angry husband had sprayed the building with gunfire, killing his own wife, kid, and one social worker.

"At that point in time," James said, "a national organization was forming, pulling in large private money to set up better facilities and networks to help the women and families relocate and get needed help, both physical and mental help. I joined the organization and helped design and set up the four clinics in this area."

"An operation of this size, to remain secret, takes some real work," Sarge said.

Pickett completely agreed with that. She couldn't even imagine the money this took.

"It takes money and good people," James said, nodding. "And everyone who works here is fully committed to the cause. They often work frighteningly long hours to help others."

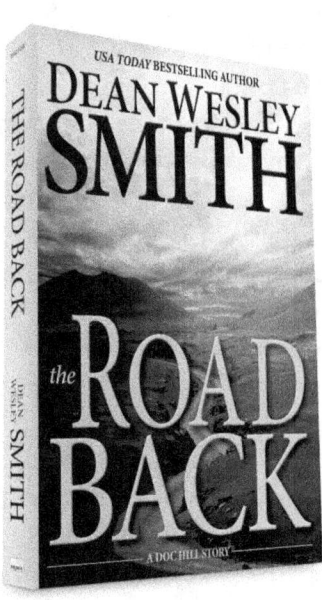

"So could you now tell us about the five sisters," Robin said.

James nodded and actually looked embarrassed. "As I said, I discovered two months ago that there is a splinter off of the national organization, one that is not sponsored or condoned in any fashion, that backs what the sisters were doing."

"And what exactly were they doing," Sarge asked.

"They were looking for the abused women who would never leave the abuser no matter how bad it got. They searched for the women trapped completely in the abuse cycle."

"And then the sisters would take care of the abuser," Robin said.

"That's what I came to understand two months ago," James said, nodding.

Pickett had to admit, James looked sick and pale even admitting that much.

"I tried to find out who they were through the national organization and no one had any idea what I was even talking about. And honestly, I believed them. This organization has nothing to do with the one that funds this place and all the others around the country."

"Who tipped you to what was happening?" Pickett asked.

"Strickland," James said. "He's worked with us from the beginning, helped in so many ways without real pay. He got the one missing person's case, Kathy Charles, that you were investigating and went deeper and discovered the death of an abuser in the woman's family."

Pickett was impressed.

Robin nodded. "I knew he was good, just didn't know how good."

"He's amazingly good," James said. "But this drove him crazy all through the summer until he managed to put all the pieces together about the five sisters,

in much the same way you three did in much faster time."

"And he brought you his findings two months ago?" Pickett asked.

James nodded. "I got so angry, I thought I was going to have a stroke."

"But neither you nor Strickland could find any evidence, could you?" Sarge asked. "Hold up in court evidence? Or even who was funding the sisters."

"Not a bit," James said. "So I called Andor and had him give you the Sandy Hunter missing person's case as a favor to me. And not say anything."

"Does Andor know what this is all about?"

"He doesn't have a clue," James said.

"So how do you know the sisters have vanished?" Robin asked.

"I called the organization's main office and told them that three detectives were investigating on the case and getting closer. Of course, the main organization claimed they had no idea what I was talking about or why I was even telling them."

Pickett nodded.

"Two days later Strickland told me that five cases of missing persons had been filed for five women, basically the five sisters. One was married, four had boyfriends. Strickland said it was the five sisters cutting and running. So I at least stopped five murders."

"That's what we were hoping to do as well," Pickett said.

"So why did you have Strickland play along instead of just coming clean with us?" Sarge asked.

"Because it has been my hope from the start that you would find these five sisters and find proof, real evidence, that they were serial killers and put them away without touching all this."

He waved his hand around at the massive room they were sitting in.

Pickett understood that.

"We know they are serial killers," Robin said.

"We know how they did it," Sarge said.

"And we know that they used Croton Oil to poison the men," Pickett said.

"But you have no proof at all, do you?" James asked, shaking his head. "Neither does Strickland."

"Not a bit beyond a little circumstantial," Sarge said. "The victims were all from families the women disappear from. One victim was seen with one woman on tape right before he died."

"Not a damn thing that would hold up in any court," Robin said. "I can tell you, it's driving Will and his people nuts as well."

"So now what do we do?" James asked.

Pickett sat back for a moment as silence filled the large space. Then she said simply, "We monitor. We combine forces and monitor."

The three looked at her like she had lost her mind.

"We have Strickland and his people," Pickett said, "we have Robin and Will and all their resources, Mike and all his resources, and we have your network here, James, nationally and all your resources. Right?"

James nodded.

"We set up searches to monitor for any known abusers suddenly dying of food poisoning. Anywhere in the country."

"Can we do that?" James asked, looking at Robin.

"We can," Robin said, nodding, clearly thinking. "But as Pickett said, we will need to combine forces. Maybe hire one or two people to work it all the time."

"I'll fund it," James said. "I feel like this has blemished all the good work we have done here in the last twenty years. I want to make up for that."

"You know," Sarge said, "chances are that we only drive these people like the sisters back into hiding every time."

"But just as we stopped five deaths here," James said, "every time we do that we can save lives. And after all, that's the point of this place."

Pickett liked that idea a lot. Usually, as a detective, you got to a scene after someone was dead. Doing this would save lives and with James' organization, help the victims of the abuse, on both sides, get help.

She liked that more than she wanted to admit.

EPILOGUE

November 24th, 2016
Las Vegas, Nevada

SARGE HANDED PICKETT two large bowls of mashed potatoes to take upstairs to the table. And then handed Robin two bowls of stuffing.

"You realize there are only five of us," Robin said, shaking her head as she followed Pickett up the stairs.

Sarge didn't care that he had made enough food to feed twenty. He loved Thanksgiving and loved cooking and didn't realize how much he missed doing it until early this morning when he got up to put in the turkey, leaving Pickett curled up under the blankets looking beautiful.

Sarge just smiled at Robin's comment. He had invited Strickland and James and his wife Patty as well, which Pickett and Robin didn't know about. So it would end up eight for his first real Thanksgiving holiday with Pickett.

Eight friends together.

The condo smelled wonderful, with the cooking turkey and baking rolls. He had gotten a big enough turkey to make sure that he and Pickett had lots of leftovers.

He glanced around for a moment, letting the turkey cool just a little more before starting to cut it.

At the moment the three kittens were stretched out in the living room on the couch, ignoring all the food and talking. To them it was just another day.

But to Sarge this day felt special. It felt like the start of something new, a new family in a way.

Pickett was coming down the stairs when someone rang the bell.

"Can you get that?" Sarge asked Pickett. "I need to carve up this monster."

"You can smell that turkey two floors down," Mike said as Pickett opened the door. Behind him was James and Patty and Strickland.

Pickett just laughed and gave them all a hug, then offered to take their coats.

Robin came back downstairs, laughed, shook her head at Sarge and went to give them hugs as well.

Sarge had felt right having them all together for the holiday. After the tour of the sanctuary and the explanation, they had spent the last few days setting up details about their new monitoring project.

It was going to take some time to find the right people to staff it and get everything in place, but it would happen. And who knows how many lives it would save.

Sarge had little hope that any real evidence would be found to catch and put

the women away, but if they kept finding them and stopping them from killing more, that would be enough for now, until the evidence did surface.

James had said that his people from the sanctuary had contacted in secret the five wives of the sister's recent targets and offered them help if needed. And James' people had set up secret monitoring in the homes to catch abuse there before it escalated into a murder.

Granted, they had not yet caught and convicted five women serial killers. But Sarge had hopes that over the years, with the monitoring program, they just might find them with evidence enough to convict them.

But on the original missing person case, the Chief of Police had been stunned that they had solved it and eighty-five total missing person cold cases at the same time.

That was a record, even for the Cold Poker Gang.

And on Tuesday night, the entire Cold Poker Gang had given the three of them a standing ovation. To Sarge, that had felt just amazing.

But it didn't beat how it felt right now, working to serve a Thanksgiving feast to some fantastic friends he hadn't even known a month ago.

And eating a wonderful holiday meal with the woman he had come to love.

The condo felt alive, felt like a home now. He would have never imagined that happening a month ago.

At that moment Pickett came into the kitchen and kissed him on the neck. "That was a wonderful surprise. Thank you."

"My pleasure," he said. "Now, as I carve the turkey, could you get the rolls out of the oven and into baskets and upstairs?"

"Gladly," Pickett said.

"But first," Sarge said, smiling at her, "tell me you love me before I go into battle with this monster beast."

"I love you," she said, laughing. "And tomorrow, let's go talk with the board about opening up that door between our places. It's time we call both of these places our home, don't you think?"

"I like that idea more than you can know," he said, smiling.

She kissed him again.

"Now, he said, "don't let the rolls burn. We have eating to do."

"And drinking," she said.

"And then pie," he said. "Can't forget pie."

"Never," she said, laughing. "Never forget the pie."

Coming Next Issue in *Smith's Monthly*

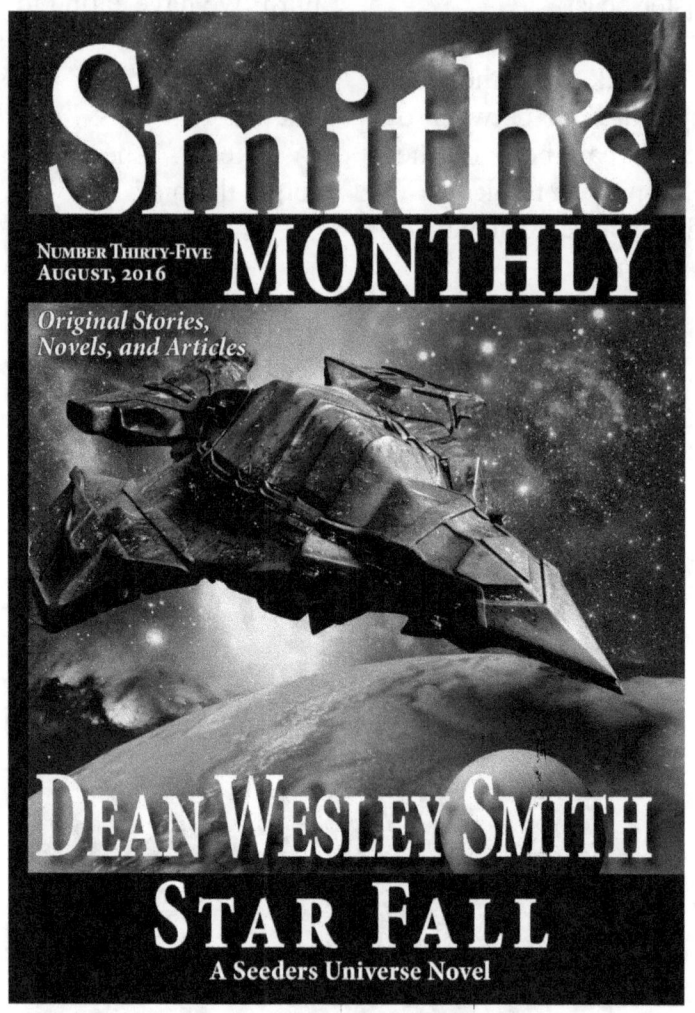

#1...October 2013

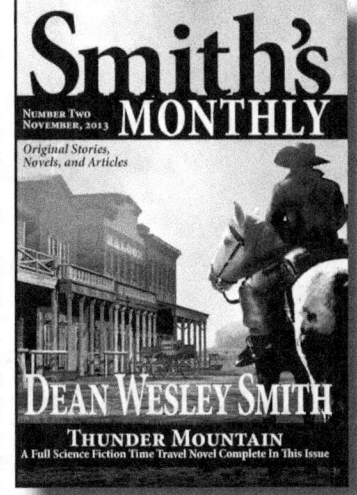

#2...November 2013

#3...December 2013

#4...January 2014

#5...February 2014

#6...March 2014

#7...April 2014

#8...May 2014

#9...June 2014

#10...July 2014

#11...August 2014

#12...September 2014

#13...October 2014

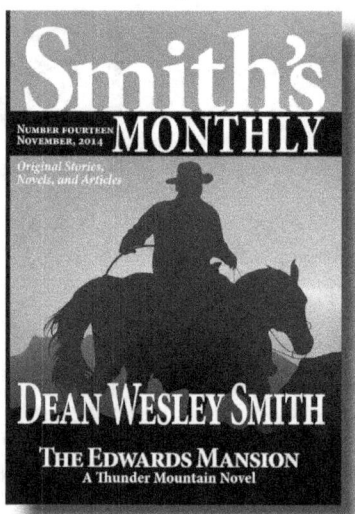

#14...November 2014

#15...December 2014

#16...January 2015

#17...February 2015

#18...March 2015

#19...April 2015

#20...May 2015

#21...June 2015

#22...July 2015

#23...August 2015

#24...September 2015

#25...October 2015

#26...November 2015

#27...December 2015

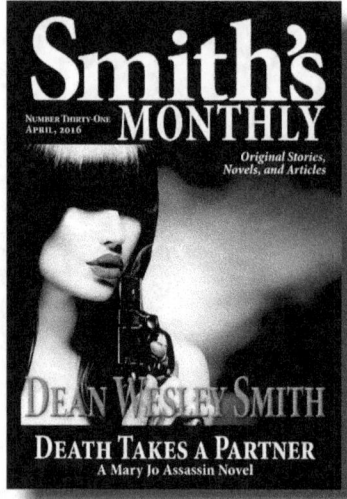

Thank You!!

I would like to thank the following wonderful people who support my blog and my work through Patreon. Your support is very important to me. Thanks!

Betsy Wilcox
Irette Y. Patterson
Kathryn Rooney
Wendy Lee Maddox
Jamie Curierre
Chris Cousino
Jane Lawson
Shantnu Tiwari
Miguel Angel Alonso Pulido
Nancy Hendrickson
Ryan M. Williams
Jacob Proffitt
Marian Goldeen
Gary Speer
Megan Bryce
Michelle Tatam
Ann Tucker
Kari Wolfe
Albert Lemke
Stacey Larson
Diane Darcy
Krystle Jones
Kari Gallagher
T. Thorn Coyle
Tasha Turner Lennhoff

Erick Lindman
Christopher Ridge
Terry Mixon
James Husun
Sherman Cox
Chong Go
Maria Grace
Grondpom
Fen
Robin Brande
J.R. Murdock
Kathleen McClure
Gunnar Gunderson
F.I. Goldhaber
Mary Jo Rabe
John Kilgallon
Dave Hendrickson
Jabberwocky
Eric Goebelbecker
Marsha Kessler
Scott Gordon
Martyn Folkes
John
Cj Lehi
Brenda Smith